FINGERPRINTS
AND
TALKING BONES

ALSO BY CHARLOTTE FOLTZ JONES

Mistakes That Worked:
40 Familiar Inventions and How They Came to Be

Accidents May Happen:
50 Inventions Discovered by Mistake

FINGERPRINTS
AND
TALKING BONES

HOW REAL-LIFE CRIMES ARE SOLVED

CHARLOTTE FOLTZ JONES

ILLUSTRATED BY DAVID G. KLEIN

**DELACORTE
PRESS**

To Bill,
who kept me on the road to Can Do

The author gratefully acknowledges Mary Cash, Laura Hornik, the Boulder City/County Citizens Police Academy, and Gerald Rosenbaugh, Colorado Bureau of Investigation.

Published by
Delacorte Press
Bantam Doubleday Dell Publishing Group, Inc.
1540 Broadway
New York, New York 10036

Library of Congress Cataloging-in-Publication Data
Jones, Charlotte Foltz.
    Fingerprints and talking bones : how real-life crimes are solved / Charlotte Foltz Jones ; illustrated by David G. Klein.
        p.   cm.
    Includes bibliographical references and index.
    Summary: Describes the many different methods used to solve crimes, including skeletal and facial reconstruction, botanical or geological information, voiceprints, and hypnosis.
    ISBN 0-385-32299-2
    1. Forensic sciences—Juvenile literature.   2. Criminal investigation—Juvenile literature.   [1. Forensic sciences.   2. Criminal investigation.]   I. Klein, David G., ill.   II. Title.
    HV8073.8.J66   1997
363.2'5—dc20   96-41277
                                                          CIP
                                                          AC

The text of this book is set in 12.5-point Sabon.
Book design by Susan Clark

Manufactured in the United States of America
June 1997
BVG   10   9   8   7   6   5   4   3   2   1

CONTENTS

INTRODUCTION

It has been said that every criminal takes something from the scene of a crime *and* leaves something behind. Often it is easy to see what was taken away—money, jewelry, even a thousand-pound safe. But discovering what was left behind requires detective work.

Fingerprints and Talking Bones is about evidence. Evidence will not stand up and leave. It will not change its mind. It will not forget. It will not get scared, nor will it make up stories. It will not get confused or excited.

The only thing about evidence that can change is its interpretation. It is up to the police not only to find the evidence but also to read it correctly to learn the truth. If the officers fail to do so, innocent people will be harmed and the guilty will go free.

All the stories in this book are true. In some cases, it might seem that solving the crime was easy, but that is not so. Crime solving takes many hours of police work, and there were usually circumstances that are not mentioned here. Law-enforcement officers use as much evidence as they can gather to convict a suspect. They have to *prove* guilt, and that is seldom possible with just one piece of evidence.

Crimes are like mysteries. There are people. There is evidence. And there are police to put all the information together and figure out "whodunit."

A NOTE TO THE READER

Is the police officer a man or a woman? Is the lab technician male or female? Was the skeleton a woman or a man?

This book often uses *he* when referring to an unnamed person. Why? Because the author believes that reading *he or she* and *him or her* is distracting and feels clumsy.

Some of the best police officers are female. Some of the finest lab technicians are women. And some of the nicest skeletons were once women. The decision to use the word *he* is not intended to diminish or ignore women. It is simply to make the text easier for you, the reader.

1

GET A CLUE!

The police arrive at the scene of a crime. How does the investigation begin? It begins with questions.

Who was involved? How? Why? Where? When? Were there witnesses? Who had a reason to commit the crime? And who had the opportunity? There might be hundreds or even thousands of questions the police have to answer before they can arrest a suspect.

The evidence answers these questions. But it takes smart officers to know what to look for and where to look. Clues can be sneaky.

GUNS

The scene of a crime is nothing like a dentist's office. Things are not quiet and peaceful. If a shot is fired, there is a *lot* of noise. Sometimes there is so much chaos that a criminal accidentally drops his gun or even tosses it aside. With a firearm as evidence, police can use its serial number to trace the owner.

But what if the shooter has erased, filed down, or scratched out the serial number? A crime lab can restore the number by using an acid or chemical etching solution. (A crime lab can also re-create an ID number on a car or motorcycle using these methods.) The numbers reappear for only a short time, though. The technician must work fast and pay careful attention.

If a suspect's gun is found away from the crime scene, police can look for evidence *inside* the gun barrel that will link the suspect to the crime. When a gun is fired near anything soft (like hair, curtains, or clothing), a vacuum occurs. Particles from the soft matter are sucked into the gun. These particles, called *blowback,* are evidence.

If a weapon is found at the scene, police look for fingerprints on the weapon, the clip, or the cartridge case. Sometimes a hair or fiber is found on the outside of the gun.

In one Colorado case, the criminal's gun fell apart at the crime scene. The criminal took most of the gun with him, but he unintentionally left behind the gun's plastic handgrip. Police identified the gun used in the crime by the handgrip.

BULLETS AND CARTRIDGES

If a criminal shoots a gun, he leaves a small gift for the police: A bullet or a spent cartridge can be traced to the gun the same way a fingerprint is traced to the finger.

When a gun is made, a hole is drilled in the barrel for the bullet to travel down. This hole is called the *bore.* The bore is drilled with spiral grooves (also called *ridges* or *rifling*). These grooves are not accidental. The spiral rifling in the bore makes the bullet spin before it leaves the gun. This keeps the bullet "gyroscopically straight" or "point first" so that it will hit its target accurately. A football spins when it is passed, using the same principle.

When a gun is fired, the firing pin hits the primer, causing the gunpowder inside the cartridge case to explode. The bullet separates from the case. The spent cartridge case remains in the chamber of a revolver. Semi-automatic guns eject the case when the gun is fired.

After the explosion inside the cartridge case, the bullet travels down the gun's barrel. As it travels, the spiral riflings mark the bullet. These grooved markings are called *striations*. The striations from one gun will differ from those caused by any other gun.

At the scene of a crime, police look for bullets and spent cartridge cases. When they find a suspect's weapon, a lab technician fires test bullets from the gun into cotton wadding or water. Under a microscope, he compares the striations on the test bullets with the marks on the bullet from the crime scene. He looks for the direction and degree of twist, the depth of the grooves, and any imperfections. If the marks match, the bullets were fired from the same gun.

The lab also examines spent cartridge cases. Every gun's firing pin hits the primer in an individual way. Its breech face (the rim that holds the cartridge in the chamber) leaves unique markings. The ejector rod (the mechanism that discharges the spent casing from the chamber) leaves distinctive marks as well. The lab can use these marks to determine whether the spent cartridge case came from the suspect's gun.

In 1976 and 1977, a man calling himself Son of Sam killed six people and wounded seven others in New York City.

When a suspect was arrested, police found a gun in his car. The crime lab proved that the bullets found in the victims' bodies had been fired from that gun. The man was tried, convicted, and sentenced to 365 years in prison.

INNOCENT BYSTANDER?

When police arrive at a crime scene, a witness might say, "I didn't do it. I got here after the guy was shot." Is this person telling the truth? Or did *he* do the shooting?

When a gun is fired, tiny specks of primer residue and gunpowder remain on the hand of the person who fired it. The police take *residue samples* from a suspect's hands, and a lab analyzes the samples for traces of the chemicals antimony, barium, and lead.

In Colorado, police arrived at a crime scene to find that a young woman had died of a gunshot wound. Two other people were at the scene. They said the woman had taken her own life. Were they telling the truth?

The police tested the hands of the two witnesses and the hands of the victim. When the results came back from the crime lab, they proved that the two witnesses were innocent. The woman had shot herself.

TOOL MARKS

You make *tool marks* in your mashed potatoes when you squish them with a fork. Tool marks are scratches, chips, scars, dents, grooves, impressions, or paint smears that a tool makes when it is forced against something softer. Police look for tool marks at a crime scene.

Most perpetrators don't realize that tools leave marks that can be traced just like fingerprints. They might use pliers to make a bomb, a shovel to scrape dirt, a crowbar to break into a safe, or a screwdriver to force open a window. When arresting a suspect, police look for tools in his vehicle or home. A crime lab can tell if the tool mark from the crime scene was made by the suspect's tool.

In one case, a burglar used wire cutters to get inside a fenced area. When police arrested a suspect, they found wire cutters in his truck. The crime lab used the suspect's tool to cut a piece of wire similar to that of the fence. The lab then magnified both pieces a thousand times. The marks the cutters made on both pieces of wire matched exactly.

When another man put a bomb on an airliner several years ago, a crime lab proved that tool marks on part of the bomb matched the jaws of a vise on the suspect's tool bench.

FIBERS

A thread is a fiber. All the tiny fragments that make up a thread are also fibers. When two pieces of fabric rub together, they leave fibers on each other. Using tape or a small handheld vacuum cleaner, police collect fibers that might be no bigger than a piece of dust. No matter how tiny the fibers are, under a microscope they can connect a suspect to a crime scene.

A woman in the South murdered her husband and put his body in the trunk of her car. She drove to the woods to hide the body. Later, when police found the man's body, they discovered tiny fibers on his clothes. They took a sample of the carpet covering on the floor of the woman's car trunk. The fibers from the car's trunk matched the fibers found on the man's clothing.

After any violent crime, police look for fibers under a victim's fingernails or on a weapon. If a burglar crawls through a window, his clothing often leaves fiber evidence behind. In hit-and-run cases, pieces of the victim's clothing are usually found caught on the car's fender, door handle, or grill.

Using a microscope, a lab can see the differences among cotton, silk, wool, acrylic, and any other type of fiber. The lab can match a small piece of fabric to a tear in the clothing of a victim or suspect. They also examine the dyes in fabrics.

Fibers are usually used with other evidence, but in a Georgia case, fibers played the crucial role. In 1979, a serial killer was terrorizing Atlanta. Police found violet and yellowish green fibers on the clothes, in the hair, and on the bodies of the victims. When police arrested a suspect in 1981, the yellowish green carpet in his home matched the fibers found on several of the victims. A violet bedspread in his home matched the violet fibers on the bodies. The man was convicted of murder in a case based largely on fiber evidence.

GLASS

Glass is glass. Right?

Wrong. Window glass is different from car windshields. Both are different from drinking glasses, eyeglasses, and bottles.

Glass taken from a suspect's clothing, shoes, or hair is sent to a crime lab and compared with glass from the crime

scene. The lab looks for thickness, color, density, and flaws. The pieces are also compared with a Refractive Index test. This test bends rays of light as they pass at an angle through the glass. If the Refractive Index test results are the same, the two pieces of glass probably came from the same source.

Surprisingly, when glass breaks, the glass showers *toward* the force, not away from it (see page 7). Sometimes pieces fly backward as much as ten feet. When police find someone covered with glass at a crime scene, he is probably the person who broke the window.

A piece of glass found on a suspect might match a missing fragment from the crime scene. This is called a *fracture match*. Making a fracture match is like piecing together parts of a jigsaw puzzle.

In one case, a thief broke a window to enter a store. He burglarized the store, then fled. Later, police put the pieces of the store window together. One piece was missing. When they arrested the suspect, they found the missing piece of glass in his pants cuff.

PAINT

Paint can chip.

Paint can smear.

Old paint can crack and break off in pieces.

Police often find chipped-off surfaces or paint-smudged tools after a break-in. Paint might be found at the crime scene or on an object in the suspect's car or home.

Paint on a bullet can prove that the bullet ricocheted off a wall before hitting a victim. A paint smear on a suspect's crowbar might match the paint on a window that was forced open during a burglary.

If a paint chip is found on a suspect, matching it like a jigsaw puzzle piece can prove that the suspect was at the scene of the crime. Paint can also be analyzed for its chemical content.

PICTURES

An old proverb says, "A picture is worth a thousand words."

After an automated teller machine (ATM) robbery, the surveillance photos were studied. They showed a car parked nearby at the time of the robbery. Soon after, the car was gone. It was the getaway car, but none of the witnesses had noticed it.

In 1991, two men robbed an armored truck in Texas. The getaway car was waiting, and the robbers probably thought they would never get caught.

Wrong!

A group of Japanese businessmen was touring the United States looking at display cases. While sitting on their tour bus, the men saw the commotion and took pictures from the bus window. Four rolls of film were turned over to the police. When the film was developed, the evidence included photos of the robbers, the getaway car, and the license plate. The police arrested the two suspects.

There are some burglars who are . . . well, not too bright!

After a man's home was burglarized in New York, police managed to retrieve his camera. When the film in the camera was developed, the photos revealed the two thieves. They had taken pictures of each other!

A similar burglary occurred in Chicago, and the thieves even forgot to take the camera with them. The owner had the roll of film developed weeks later and found pictures of two strangers. The setting was familiar, though. She realized they must be the thieves! They had taken pictures of each other while burglarizing her house!

SHOE PRINTS

Many criminals don't realize that their own feet can betray them.

Shoe manufacturers make thousands of identical shoes. But since everyone's walking style is individual, each shoe wears differently. Any scratch, nick, cut, or other damage mark in the sole makes a shoe one of a kind.

If a burglar's shoes have oil, grease, blood, grass stains, or soil on them, he will likely leave shoe tracks. Police often find shoe prints on kicked-in doors after a theft.

A burglar in Philadelphia left a dirty sneaker print on an apartment wall while he was stealing a stereo and a VCR. When police arrested him, his shoe matched the print perfectly.

In New York, a man murdered the manager of a clothing store. He left behind a bloody shoe print. The Federal Bureau of Investigation (FBI) proved the print came from the suspect's shoe, and he was convicted of the murder.

Latent shoe prints (prints that can't be seen by the naked eye) are more difficult to find, but sometimes they can be electrically lifted. In a bank holdup, the robber scrambled over the counter. Police used a *static dust lifter* to collect the shoe prints. This device works by spreading aluminum foil

over the print and applying fifteen thousand volts of electricity to the foil. The electricity makes the print stick to the aluminum foil. When the suspect was arrested, his shoes matched the prints from the bank counter.

If a burglar enters a house through a window, he might step in the soft dirt of a flower bed. Or he might walk through mud, sand, or even snow. When police find shoe impressions, they photograph, measure, and sketch them. They make a mold by pouring plaster or dental stone-casting solution over the marks. Police have special wax to take shoe impressions left in snow.

It's not always shoe *prints* that help the police. In Charles City, Virginia, police chased a suspected drug dealer through the woods. The man was wearing shoes with red lights built into the heels. Every time his foot hit the ground, the lights flashed. The officers simply followed the flashing lights until they caught the suspect.

DOCUMENT ANALYSIS

Document analysis sounds complicated. In truth, it simply means answering questions, such as "Who really signed the contract?" or "Did someone alter the amount of the check?" or "Which typewriter was used to type the manifesto?"

A woman in Oklahoma transferred money out of a man's bank account and changed his car title to her name. Then she killed the man. Police couldn't prove she had killed him until they proved she had forged his signature. She was convicted of murder and is now in prison.

Document experts prove forgeries such as this one by enlarging both the questioned signature and a known (un-

fingerprints and talking bones
and fingerprints and talking
bones fingerprints and
bones s and fingerprints
talking ones and finger-
king bones and
and tall nd talking
prints erprints and
finger and fingerprints

forged) signature. They compare the two, looking for breaks in the pen stroke, pauses, crossed letters, or dotted letters.

Some forgeries involve the changing of a document's amount. By closing in the 3s, for example, a criminal can change $333 into $888 on a contract, sales ticket, or other legal document. If the perpetrator thinks his pen's ink matches the original ink used to write the document, he's wrong. Crime labs have special lights to show that the inks came from different pens.

Sometimes extra words or phrases are added to contracts,

wills, or deeds. Experts can test for this sort of forgery by placing a grid over the text (see page 13). The grid detects letters that were not formed by the same machine and words or lines that were added after the printing of the original document.

A rare-documents dealer in Utah forged papers detailing his church's history. He then killed two people to cover up his initial crime. In solving the two murders, police uncovered the forged documents and used them to identify the perpetrator. The man is now in prison.

Beginning in 1978, a man referred to in the media as the Unabomber killed three people and injured twenty-three others with homemade bombs. In 1995, the perpetrator sent an essay called the "Manifesto" to two large newspapers and demanded they publish it. When a suspect was arrested in 1996, authorities matched the typing of the "Manifesto" with a typewriter in the suspect's cabin. They looked for spacing, alignment, and nicks in the letters. They confirmed that one of the suspect's typewriters had been used to type the "Manifesto" by comparing the way each letter was formed.

SIGNATURE AND M.O.

Sounds silly, doesn't it? Why would a criminal stop and sign his name at the crime scene?

While most criminals don't actually sign their name, they leave evidence that police call a *signature*. Burglars might use the same tools to break into a number of houses and leave the same tool marks behind. Serial killers often use the same method of killing. Bombers may make their bombs in the same style using the same kinds of materials.

The Unabomber sent sixteen bombs between 1978 and 1995. He made all his bombs in the same way, and he even stamped the initials *FC* into a piece of metal on each bomb. Other people mailed bombs during those same eighteen years, but the FBI knew that those bombs had not been made by the Unabomber. They were constructed differently—they didn't have his signature.

Police also refer to an M.O., which is the abbreviation of the Latin phrase *modus operandi*, meaning "method of operating." A signature refers to the small things a perpetrator does during each crime that make him different. An M.O. is the entire way a criminal commits a crime.

One robber's M.O. was always stealing from the same fast-food chain; always jumping over the counter; and always asking the cashier, "Have you ever been shot?"

A Denver burglar's M.O. earned him the title the Human Fly. Wearing all black, he scaled the sides of high-rise apartment buildings and entered people's apartments while they were sleeping.

TRASH

Call it *trash* if you will, but litter often holds important clues.

Cigarette butts, candy and gum wrappers, newspapers, gift wrap, paper bags, and even used tissues can link a person to the scene of a crime.

In a California case, police found part of a chewing gum wrapper at a crime scene. When a suspect was arrested, he had part of the same chewing gum wrapper in his pocket. Police fitted the two pieces together. They matched perfectly, proving that the suspect had been at the scene of the crime.

Explosives always leave evidence. After an explosion, police might find blasting-cap fragments, detonating wire, safety fuses, dynamite paper, cotton, soap, masking tape, Primacord, steel fragments, and samples of unexploded materials. This trash is checked for fingerprints, traced to matching material at the suspect's home, or traced to the dealer who sold the materials.

After a burglary, insulation from a safe can be identified under a microscope. Since people don't usually go around wearing safe insulation, finding it on a person's clothes or shoes is a strong indication of guilt. The crime lab then looks for color, mineral content, and physical appearance to match the evidence with insulation from the crime scene.

There is a famous story of an officer who arrested a man for a minor violation and took him to police headquarters. The officer felt sorry for the poor guy because he had a terrible case of dandruff. But the longer the officer looked at the dandruff on the man's jacket, the more suspicious he became. He had the dandruff analyzed and found that the guy had just blown up a safe.

About 90% of local police agencies have fewer than 25 sworn officers.

New York City has the largest police department, with more than 30,000 sworn officers.

Almost half the police departments in the United States have fewer than 10 sworn officers.

There are more than 561,500 sworn law-enforcement officers in the United States.

U.S. CRIME CLOCK

A property crime is committed every 3 seconds.

2

CARS CONFESSING

Cars tell police more than their drivers realize.

Witnesses often write down license plate numbers that lead police to a suspect. The make, model, and year of the car help track it.

But even if there are no witnesses, a crime can be solved using evidence left behind by the criminal's car.

CAR PAINT

When a man in Florida robbed a bank, he rushed out to his car to make a fast getaway. As he pulled out of his parking place, *crash!* The robber smashed into the parking meter. He escaped, but he left a sample of his car's paint on the meter. A paint expert identified the exact color and type of paint, which told him the make and year of the automobile. Police located the suspect through vehicle registrations.

A paint chip left at a crime scene might be small, but once it is placed under the microscope, it tells the story of the car. If the car has been repainted, the crime lab identifies the vehicle from the factory's original layer of paint.

One crime lab received a scraping from a car that had been repainted six times. The police found the car and were fairly certain of their suspect. How many cars, after all, would have the same six colors painted in the same order?

Paint is often a clue in hit-and-run accidents. If a car hits a bicycle, a person, or another car, paint is usually left on the other vehicle or in the fibers of clothing.

If the paint chip is large enough, it can be matched to a chipped spot on the suspect's car—sort of like a jigsaw puzzle.

TIRES

Two different types of tire tracks help police trace a criminal.

Contamination prints are made when a car drives through a substance such as oil, blood, paint, or mud. The tire then leaves a print on the street or driveway. Skid marks are also contamination prints.

An *impression print* is made by a vehicle when it drives through something soft (like mud or sand).

If the police find tire tracks, they photograph, measure, and sketch them. For impression prints, they make a plaster cast in the same fashion as shoe print molds.

By measuring the width of the tire track and the distance between the tires, police can tell the size of the vehicle. The tires of a large pickup truck will make different tracks from those of a small car.

After two murders in California, police asked an expert to identify the tire print. The print had been made by a very expensive tire. When a suspect was arrested, his tires matched the tracks from the crime scene.

As with the soles of shoes, every tire is different. Although thousands appear to be the same, each tire has small flaws. Once the tire is on a vehicle, every sharp object in the road nicks it. Sometimes a small stone is embedded in the tread, or the tire might have a nail puncture repair. Tires also wear differently, depending on air pressure and front-end alignment. Everything that happens to a tire makes that tire's print individual. When a suspect is apprehended, the tire track can help prove his presence at the scene of a crime.

SPARE PARTS

After a hit-and-run accident in Colorado, police found a red taillight lens at the scene. Inside the lens was a number. The crime lab found a car expert in Japan who provided information about the make (it was a Toyota), the style (a small pickup), and the span of years when the lens was installed on the vehicle.

In another Colorado hit-and-run case, the car's bumper came off on impact. From the bumper, police identified the make, model, year, and color of the car. It was a luxury car, and the local dealer provided a list of people who had purchased that particular make. Police found the car and had a suspect.

DIRTY OIL

Police questioned a suspect in a hit-and-run accident. The man said his car was in the shop having its oil changed at the time of the accident. The lab analyzed a sample of the car's oil and found that it had not been changed for four thousand miles. The man's alibi collapsed, and he was arrested.

No License Plates

In 1995, an Oklahoma state trooper stopped a car because it had no license plates. The driver was arrested (on charges of driving without tags, driving without insurance, and carrying a concealed weapon). He stayed in jail for two days. Just minutes before he was to be released, the jail received a call from the FBI telling them to hold the prisoner. He was a suspect in the bombing of the Oklahoma City Federal Building.

In another case, New York state troopers stopped a pickup that had no license plates. After noticing a terrible odor coming from the truck, one of the troopers found a woman's body in the back. The driver confessed to seventeen murders.

Parking Ticket

In 1977, a gunman known as Son of Sam had killed six people in New York City. One night, a woman who was out walking her dog saw a police officer putting a ticket on a car. Minutes later, a suspicious man approached her. He looked directly into her face, then passed. He held his right arm stiffly, as though he might be carrying a gun up his sleeve. The woman was frightened and ran home, but while she was on her porch, she heard gunshots.

The next day the woman learned of the double shooting near her home, and she felt certain the passing stranger had been the killer.

When she called the police, she remembered another detail that turned out to be very important: She had seen a police officer ticketing a car parked illegally near a fire hydrant one block from the murder site.

The police traced all the parking tickets issued in the area. One such ticket belonged to a man who lived twenty-five miles away. What was his car doing so far from home at two-thirty in the morning? Police traced the car. They peered inside it and saw a weapon in the backseat. They also saw a letter like the ones the killer had been sending to the police.

The police arrested the man. He was identified as Son of Sam and convicted of the murders.

DEAD BATTERY

On a cold December night in 1990, a man entered a fast-food restaurant in Olathe, Kansas. He robbed the employees and put them in the restaurant's cooler. Then he escaped.

After the man left, the manager got out of the cooler and called the police.

A few minutes later, the robber returned to the restaurant. The temperature outside was below zero and his car battery was dead. He needed the manager to help him jump-start his engine.

When the police arrived, the manager and the robber were in the parking lot working on the car.

FASCINATING U.S. CRIME FACTS

About 43.5 million crimes are committed each year.

There are 195,900 arrests made for motor vehicle theft each year.

The U.S. crime rate has been dropping for the last 20 years.

The most common reason for arrest in the United States is "driving under the influence."

U.S. CRIME CLOCK

A motor vehicle theft occurs every 20 seconds.

3

BODY LANGUAGE

What does every criminal bring to the scene of a crime? His fingers. His hair. His blood. His teeth. His voice. Little does he imagine that his own body parts may help convict him.

The Fifth Amendment of the United States Constitution says that a person cannot be forced to testify against himself. No one can make him say, "I did it." *But* there is nothing in the Constitution stating that his body can't be used against him in court. A person's body can provide a lot of surprising and revealing information.

BITE MARKS

A basic instinct in animals is to use their teeth in self-defense or battle. Small children often show their aggression by biting. And many criminals use their teeth when committing a crime.

If police find a bite mark on a victim, a forensic odontologist is called in to make a cast or model of the mark. He takes photographs and X rays and creates computer enhancements. When a suspect is arrested, plaster models are made of his teeth.

The odontologist compares the suspect's teeth with the bite mark. He notes the size and shape of the teeth. He looks for crooked, jagged, or missing teeth, ridges, fillings, chips,

grooves, space between teeth, and other imperfections. Everyone's bite is unique. Even people with perfect teeth or false teeth have a distinctive bite.

In 1978, a suspect was arrested in Florida for killing two college women and a twelve-year-old girl. Police found bite marks on one of the college women. An odontologist identified the bite marks as the suspect's. His lower teeth were jagged, and the expert said that his teeth matched the bite mark "almost like a key fitting in a lock." The teeth marks were the proof needed for a conviction. The man admitted he had killed other women across the United States, and he was later given the death sentence.

One of the first cases to use teeth marks as evidence was solved in Texas more than forty years ago. A man robbed a grocery store. As he left, he took a bite out of a piece of cheese. The police later arrested a suspect, and his teeth matched the bite marks in the cheese perfectly.

Bite marks can eliminate the innocent from suspicion. In a California case, police found a wad of chewing gum at the scene of a murder. After two suspects had been arrested, an odontologist took dental impressions of them and of the victim. One of the suspects had a root canal on a back tooth that matched the impression in the gum perfectly. The suspect's saliva also matched the blood type of the saliva in the gum. The man pleaded guilty to second-degree murder.

FINGERNAIL MARKS

Just as experts can identify a bullet from a certain gun, they can match the lines on a broken fingernail under a microscope to tell if it came from a certain finger.

In an unusual Pennsylvania case, after two children were killed, fingernail marks were found on one victim's neck. When a suspect was arrested, an odontologist was able to apply his professional knowledge toward identifying the nail marks on the child as matching the suspect's fingernails. The fingernail evidence did not convict the suspect, but it was used as part of the case against him.

In violent crimes, victims often scratch their attacker. Police check under a victim's fingernails for skin tissue.

BLOOD

Blood, one of the most common types of evidence found at the scene of a violent crime, follows certain laws of physics.

The splatters of blood on a wall might have a point. This point indicates the direction in which the blood was moving. Investigators use this information to analyze where the victim was and which direction the attack came from. (This is part of *reconstructing* the crime scene.)

A drop of blood that falls a long way splashes. There will be lines away from the main drop, sort of like sun rays. If the blood drop is round or oval, it probably fell only a few inches. Another law of physics dictates the size of blood drops. Large drops mean the person was probably hit— perhaps by a fist to the nose. If each drop of blood in a sequence is smaller than the last, the victim might have been stabbed. If the victim was hit by a bullet, the blood droplets will be tiny—almost like a mist.

Blood evidence is collected carefully and taken to a crime lab. First it is determined whether the evidence truly is blood. Paint, chemicals, or rust mixed with water can look like blood. The sample is then tested to see if it comes from a human or an animal.

Human blood is typed. A person inherits his blood type from his parents and keeps that type throughout his life. Everyone has one of four blood types: A, B, AB, or O. Type O is the most common. Type A is the second most common, followed by Type B. Type AB is the rarest.

Since there are only four blood types, millions of people share each type. Matching blood type alone doesn't prove a suspect's guilt. But blood also contains enzymes and proteins, and each person's chemicals are different. A lab can identify the enzymes and proteins in a blood sample. There is only a small chance that two people would have the same blood type *and* the same chemical combination.

A case in Colorado was solved almost entirely with blood evidence. The bodies of a young man and an elderly woman were found in a house. Had the man killed the woman and then himself? Or had the woman killed the man and then herself? Or had someone else killed both of them? Police reconstructed the crime scene and examined the blood evidence. They found microscopic drops of the man's blood on the woman's glasses. From that they concluded that the woman had killed the young man and then killed herself.

Until recently, traditional blood tests were the only way of linking a suspect to a crime. In the 1980s, a new test was discovered called DNA testing. There's more about DNA in chapter 8.

BODY FLUIDS

Amazing as it seems, the body is made up of 92 percent water or fluid. The body's fluids—blood, sweat, saliva, semen, and urine—can all be useful in crime investigation.

Most people are *secretors*. That means their blood type is also present in their body fluids. If police find a cigarette butt or a sweat-stained hat, the crime lab can identify the suspect's blood type from the dried saliva or sweat.

DNA testing can be done on body fluids as well as blood.

FINGERPRINTS, TOE PRINTS, AND PALM PRINTS

About three or four months before you were born, tiny ridges formed on your fingers, toes, hands, and feet. No matter how big or old you get, those ridges will not go away. They will get larger as you grow, but the pattern will never change.

The prints on each finger, toe, and palm are different, and no two people—not even identical twins—have the same pattern. One expert figured that the circumstance of two persons' having the same fingerprints would happen only once in 466,037,700 years.

Most criminals wear shoes to a crime scene, so toe print evidence is rarely found. But occasionally a burglar will remove his shoes and put his socks over his hands so that he won't leave fingerprints behind. He doesn't realize that if he's arrested, police can identify him by his toe prints.

The uniqueness of fingerprints was first recognized centuries ago. In 1900, Sir Edward R. Henry set up a fingerprinting system for identifying criminals in England. The FBI's Identification Division was started in 1924 with only 810,000 fingerprint cards. Today the FBI's computerized system contains more than 200 million fingerprints.

FINGERPRINTS AT THE CRIME SCENE

There are three different types of fingerprints that police look for at a crime scene:

- **Visible (or patent) prints** are easily seen by the naked eye. A perpetrator who has dirt, blood, grease, or food on his fingers during the crime will leave visible prints.

- **Plastic prints** are those that leave an impression—for example, in chocolate, paint, glue, or another pliable substance.

- **Latent prints** are invisible. They are formed when perspiration and oils are secreted from small pores on the ridges of the fingerprint.

When police approach a crime scene, they estimate where the perpetrator placed his hands to gain entry and commit the crime. If there are no visible prints there, they look for latent prints.

There are at least forty ways to develop fingerprints.

On glass, plastic, metal, or other hard surfaces, police dust for prints. The fine dusting powder clings to the perspiration. An officer brushes away excess powder, photographs the fingerprint, then "lifts" it with a sticky tape.

The fuming method finds prints on plastics, aluminum foil, wood, rubber, vinyl, leather, bricks, plasterboard, smooth rocks, guns, and in some cases, on the bodies of victims. It works by heating cyanoacrylate (the sticky substance used to make Super Glue). The substance evaporates, and the vapor clings to fingerprint moisture, forming hard, visible ridges. There's one problem with this method—the residue is impossible to remove. Anything that comes in contact with the fumes is usable only as evidence.

The chemical method, incorporating iodine, ninhydrin, and silver nitrate, is used on porous surfaces such as cardboard and paper.

Police also use special lights to collect fingerprints. Laser light rays do not spread. When a laser beam hits the sweat and body oils of a fingerprint, the intense light makes the print fluorescent. As one expert says, "A fingerprint glows like a firefly!"

Some departments use an Alternate Light Source (ALS). In a dark room, this high-intensity arc light with special filters makes latent fingerprints (as well as body fluids) appear like magic.

Prints have been found in some very unusual places. After an armored-car robbery in Pennsylvania, one fingerprint was found inside a toilet paper roll that had been used to replace the money in a money bag.

In Georgia, a murderer's fingerprint was found inside the victim's purse.

And in New York, a suspect was apprehended when police found his fingerprint in a phone book beside a murder victim's name and address.

COLLECTING FINGERPRINTS
FROM SUSPECTS

For almost a hundred years police took a suspect's finger-prints by rolling each finger in black ink and pressing the finger onto a card. The procedure took twenty minutes, and the cards often got smudged.

Some police departments now have optical scanners that take prints in a flash. The officer rolls a suspect's fingers on top of a glass scanner. Video cameras record the finger-prints. The computer converts them into a number code. Then the prints are stored in the computer—all in less than five minutes.

Not everyone likes the optical scanners. Dirt on the glass screen or on the suspect's fingers can cause the computer to read the dirt, thus misreading the fingerprint.

IDENTIFYING FINGERPRINTS

Until the 1980s, the process of fingerprint identification was tedious and time-consuming. Police would search through file cabinets of thousands of fingerprints that had been taken from people arrested earlier. They would com-pare the prints on file with the fingerprints from the scene, looking for loops, arches, and whorls. Under those three classifications are eight subclassifications: plain whorl, radial loop, plain arch, double loop, ulnar loop, tented arch, accidental whorl, and central pocket loop.

The computer has allowed for a simplified process: the Automated Fingerprint Identification System (AFIS). AFIS electronically compares prints from a crime scene with the

prints in its files and lists the likely matches. An officer then makes the final comparison.

Depending on the system, AFIS can scan 500 to 1,200 prints per second. The more information the computer has, the faster the search goes. For instance, if it is known that the suspect is male, all the females' prints can be eliminated. If a witness has identified the suspect's race, all other races are eliminated. Sometimes an unidentified print can be checked against a million stored prints in less than forty-five minutes—a job that would take an officer seventeen thousand hours to do by hand.

A forty-eight-year-old woman was killed in San Francisco in 1978. Officers went through three hundred thousand fingerprint cards trying to find the killer—with no success. In 1985, the city installed AFIS. Within six minutes, the computer identified a man who had once been arrested for trespassing. The man pleaded guilty to first-degree murder.

One disadvantage of the AFIS system is its price. The most basic system costs about $2 million. New York State's system cost $40 million. But the results are miraculous.

A New York City woman was murdered in 1974. Police found fingerprints on a drinking glass and on a window, but they could not make a match. In 1992, a detective ran the fingerprints through a national computer database and matched them with a suspect. Eighteen years after the crime, the suspect was arrested in South Carolina and finally convicted.

In 1963, a middle-aged woman was murdered in Los Angeles. The perpetrator left thirty-six fingerprints around the victim's apartment. Police searched their files but could not match the fingerprints to anyone they had arrested before.

Twenty-seven years later, the Los Angeles police department purchased an AFIS computer. They ran the fingerprints from the 1963 murder scene through the computer. It came up with a name. The man was arrested, tried in 1993, and convicted for the murder—thirty years after it had happened.

LIP PRINTS

Lip prints will never be as helpful as fingerprints. After all, not every criminal takes time for a drink while committing a crime! But lip printing research has been done in Japan, and as one expert has said, police "must look at any new method that provides the evidence necessary to gain convictions."

Lip prints also contain saliva, which can be used in blood typing and DNA testing.

HAIR

When someone focuses excessively on details, it's said that he's "splitting hairs."

"Splitting hairs" is exactly what police do.

Hair grows about a half inch per month and falls out regularly, so police often find a suspect's hair at a crime scene. From one strand of hair, the crime lab can determine the following:

• whether it comes from an animal or a human

• the race of the person the hair belongs to

• whether the hair fell out or was pulled out

- what drugs the person is taking and when they were used

- the chemical makeup of the person's hair

- whether the person has certain diseases

- what part of the body the hair comes from

- whether the hair is real or from a wig

- whether the hair has been dyed or bleached

If the root of a hair is attached, DNA tests can be run. And sometimes the hair provides a clue to the person's age and sex.

Though police can learn all these things from a hair, they cannot use it to positively identify a suspect. However, they can show that the hair *could* have come from the suspect. They can also prove that the hair did *not* come from a certain person, thus eliminating an innocent suspect.

Hair played an important part in drug charges filed against the mayor of a large city. Police had proof that he had used illegal drugs during the three days before his arrest, but they needed to prove that he had a *habit* of drug use. The crime lab's hair test showed that he had been using cocaine for as long as the hair on his head had been growing.

PET HAIR

Even Fido's hair can be used as evidence. If a suspect is caught with the hair of a victim's pet on his clothes, that evidence can be used against him.

In one case, a young woman looked out her window in

37

time to see someone murder her boyfriend, then ride away on a bicycle. She couldn't see the killer's face. When the police arrived, they found white hair on the victim's jacket. The young woman remembered that an ex-boyfriend of hers had a white Samoyed dog.

The crime lab examined the white hair on the victim's jacket and determined that it probably came from the ex-boyfriend's dog. The suspect was convicted of murder.

HYPNOSIS

Experts continue to debate the validity of hypnosis as a crime-solving tool. Some say it can help a person remember details that have been clouded by shock. Others claim that hypnosis confuses subjects into regarding their fantasies as truth.

Many states do not allow hypnosis as evidence in their courts. Occasionally, though, hypnosis is used on witnesses whose court testimony will not be necessary.

When an Arkansas woman was charged with killing her husband, she could not recall the details of the shooting. Once under hypnosis, she remembered that her finger was *not* on the trigger when the gun fired. She also remembered that the gun went off when her husband grabbed her arm. The case went to the United States Supreme Court. That court ruled that she could testify about her hypnotically refreshed memory.

PSYCHOLOGICAL PROFILE

Psychologists can tell an astonishing number of things about a suspect by analyzing the crime scene. If the scene is neat, the killer is probably neat. If the act involved more violence than necessary, the killer probably knew his victim. And if the killing took place during the day, the killer was probably from the area. They can also determine the following:

- the killer's approximate age, sex, and race

- how he was raised

- whether he is married

- his level of education

- aspects of his personality

- his lifestyle and habits

- whether he has friends or is a loner

- whether he has a criminal history

- sometimes, his motive for committing the crime

- what he might do next

In one of the first cases to use a psychological profile, a criminal known as the Mad Bomber terrorized New York City in the 1940s and 1950s by setting bombs in train stations and theaters. A psychiatrist developed a description of the bomber. When the man was arrested, the description matched—right down to the fact that he wore a double-breasted suit!

In a Nebraska case, psychologists told police that the killer of two boys was nineteen to twenty-two years old (he was twenty);

was less than five feet, three inches tall (he was four feet, four inches tall);

weighed 140 to 150 pounds (he weighed 140 pounds);

worked the night shift doing menial labor (he did night-time maintenance work);

was unmarried (he was single); and

drove a bland, midsize car with high mileage (he drove a beige car with high mileage).

The psychologists' profile described the perpetrator almost exactly.

The FBI tried to identify the Unabomber using five different psychological profiles. All five profiles agreed that he was a loner. When a suspect was arrested in 1996, he was in fact a recluse living miles from civilization. Through the years, the profiles had become more accurate. The later ones also said that the Unabomber

grew up in the Chicago area (the suspect did);

had ties to Salt Lake City (he worked there for a short time);

had ties to the San Francisco area (he taught near there);

was intelligent (he had a doctoral degree in mathematics); and

was a white male in his fifties (he was a fifty-three-year-old white male).

Only one assumption was wrong. Since no bombs were sent between 1987 and 1993, it was thought that the Unabomber was in prison during that time. When the suspect was identified, he had no previous arrest record.

STOMACH CONTENTS

Go ahead and say, "Ick!" Crime solving can sometimes be disgusting work.

Food in a murder victim's stomach tells a lot about his last hours of life. If hamburgers and french fries are in the stomach, he probably ate at a fast-food restaurant. Employees at nearby restaurants might remember seeing the victim and even have information on whom he was with. (Most victims are killed by someone they know.)

In one case, a pizza deliveryman had delivered pizzas to two different apartments. When the residents of one apartment were found murdered, the deliveryman came forward. He remembered the deliveries but not the people who were in each apartment. When the victims' stomachs were analyzed, onion pizza was found. That was the clue that jogged the deliveryman's memory. He matched the order to the people in the apartment and was able to describe them all—including the perpetrator.

A crime scene is stressful and full of chaos. When some people become agitated, they throw up. Vomit at a crime scene might be from the victim *or* the perpetrator. Police can have the vomit analyzed and also have DNA testing done.

A medical pathologist made a surprise discovery during the autopsy of a Michigan man—but it wasn't food! The man had died of heart trouble, but the pathologist found a diamond ring in his intestines. Police traced the $35,000 ring to a New York jeweler. The man had stolen the ring a year earlier, then swallowed it when he was arrested.

VOICEPRINTS

A spectograph turns speech sounds into pictures that are measured on graph paper. This process is similar to the way electronic impulses are turned into television images.

Every person's voice is different. To speak even one word requires the vocal cords, palate, tongue, teeth, lips, nose, sinuses, and throat and jaw muscles. The pitches and the way people say certain letters and words cannot be changed. Even when a person disguises his voice, it does not change the way those muscles work, and it cannot fool a voiceprint.

Sometimes telephone calls are taped, an answering machine message is saved, or a surveillance camera records a voice. If police make an arrest, they can take a voice sample from the suspect. Using a spectograph machine, the voices from the crime scene are compared with the suspect's voice.

Spectograph results are not always accepted in trials. Police need additional evidence. But a voiceprint can help police recognize whether or not they have the right person.

After a Texas convenience store robbery and murder, police arrested a suspect who looked like the man on the surveillance tape. A voiceprint expert compared the suspect's voice with the one on the tape and determined that the suspect was *not* the person who had killed the clerk. The man was released and happily went home.

There are 23,400 arrests made for murder each year.

California has the most murders, with more than 3,700 each year.

About 70% of murders are committed with a firearm.

North Dakota has the fewest murders. In one recent year, the state had only one.

U.S. CRIME CLOCK

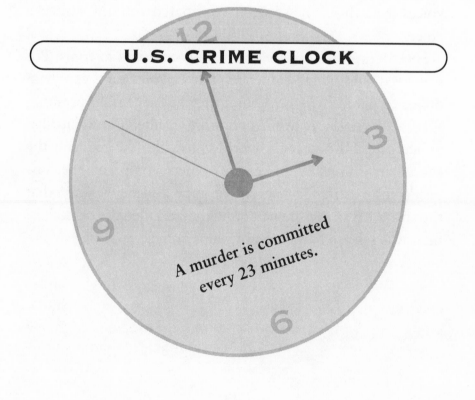

A murder is committed every 23 minutes.

4

SKELETONS TALKING

Skeletons talking? Do they yell or whisper? Do they speak English or French or Japanese? And what do they have to say?

Of course, everyone knows skeletons can't talk—at least not in the way we think of language. But if talking means conveying a message, then skeletons *can* talk. There are 206 bones and 32 teeth in the human body. When a skeleton is found, each bone and tooth has a tale to tell.

FORENSIC ANTHROPOLOGISTS

Forensic anthropologists examine dead bodies when the soft tissue (skin and organs) is gone. They work with bones and connective tissue (such as joints). They identify bodies that have been burned or damaged beyond recognition, such as in an airplane crash. They can determine details of the dead person's life, as well as the cause of death.

Sometimes the forensic anthropologist goes to the scene of the crime, but more often the bones are delivered to his lab. There are only about fifty forensic anthropologists in the United States.

To most people, bones look like . . . well, bones. So an anthropologist must first determine whether the skeleton parts are human or animal. An Oklahoma highway patrolman found part of a skeleton beside a highway. An

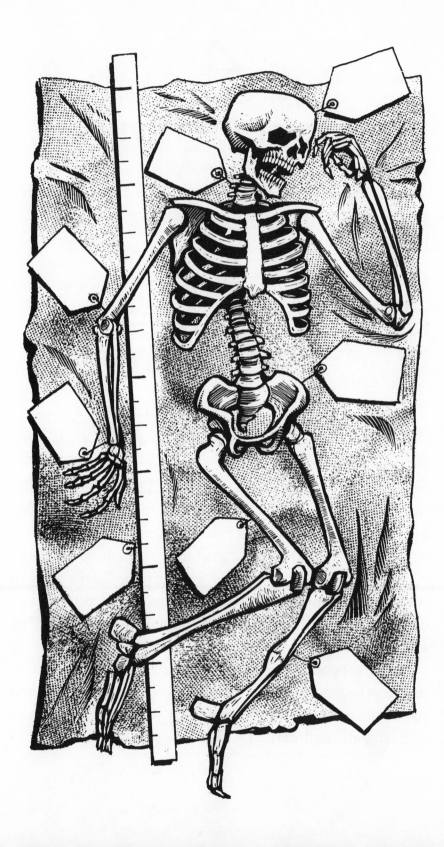

anthropologist examined the bones and was happy to report that they had belonged to a calf!

But when the bones are human, a forensic anthropologist's work has just begun. He must "interview" the skeleton; he must make that skeleton talk. What might the skeleton say?

- **Whether the person was male or female.** This is judged by examining the pelvis, the base of the skull, the forehead, and the jaw—males have a heavier, more prominent brow ridge, and the jaw is usually squared off.

- **Approximately how old he was.** This is determined by examining the joints, bones, and teeth. Part of a child's skull is open to allow room for growth. The smoother the skull, the older the person.

- **How tall he was.** A formula determines probable height based on the length of the long leg bones and the arm bones.

- **Whether he was thin or heavy.** His weight will have affected the wear on the bones at certain points.

- **What racial group he belonged to.** This is determined by examining the width and height of the nose. Facial or head hair, when found with the skeleton, can also help pinpoint race.

- **What his occupation was.** If a person played an instrument such as a flute or clarinet, the teeth and the bones around the mouth will be affected. A carpenter's or a roofer's teeth will be chipped in front where he held nails in his mouth.

- **How he was shaped.** Ridges where muscle was attached to the bone show the person's physique.

- **Whether he was right-handed or left-handed.** Again, there will have been more muscle attachment to the bones on the side where the person used his arm and hand more.

- **Whether he had been injured during his lifetime.** Detected bone injuries can be compared with a person's medical X rays to confirm identity.

- **Whether he died violently.** This is determined by looking for signs of trauma such as stab marks, marks on the skull, broken bones, or bullets or pellets in or near the body. If the person was strangled, the bone from the throat (the hyoid bone) will be fractured.

- **When he died.** The amount of soft tissue that is still present can be considered.

Sometimes identification goes quickly. More often each skeleton takes months of work. In one case, an anthropologist was sent a box of bones to identify after a murder and suicide in a shed. A man had killed his girlfriend, then set the shed on fire, then killed himself. All the bones were burned. To further complicate the case, a dog had been inside the shed when it burned, so there were dog bones mixed in with the human bones. Instead of keeping each body's bones separate, an investigator put everything in one body bag. By the time the bones arrived at the anthropologist's lab, they were completely jumbled. There were ten thousand bone fragments, and it took a year and a half to reassemble the pieces.

RECONSTRUCTION

The police find a skeleton but have no idea who the guy was. How do they make an identification? First, the skeleton needs a face.

Sometimes forensic anthropologists do the artwork of creating a face for a skeleton. Others team up with an artist. A forensic artist creates a *three-dimensional facial reproduction*. He molds clay directly over the skull and mandible (the lower jawbone) to create a face. Sometimes a plaster cast is made of the skull and the clay is formed over the cast.

The anthropologist determines as much as possible from the skeleton—age, race, sex. Then, using *tissue thickness charts,* the artist glues pieces of pencil erasers to the skull at eighteen to twenty-six key points. These pegs are cut to the thicknesses specified by the chart.

Using the pegs as a guide, the artist fills in the areas between them with layers of modeling clay. Eyes are the most difficult part to do, since they are formed entirely by tissue. Eyes might be large or small or squinty or deep-set.

Other difficult areas are the eyelids, the lower parts of the nose, the lips, and the ears. The artist works from his own knowledge of people's faces and from his artistic experience.

A wig matched to hair from the body's remains is placed on the completed head.

TEETH

Teeth were discussed in chapter 3 in the "Bite Marks" section. But teeth don't have to bite to be helpful. Teeth help identify victims of plane crashes and other catastrophes, as well as crime victims. Fingerprints and DNA are used where possible, but teeth (sometimes a single tooth) can also lead to an identification.

An odontologist compares the victim's teeth with dental records. When a plane crashes, 75 percent of the victims are identified by their dental records. And since teeth are the most durable part of the body, they can be helpful even after many years.

Before the authorities know who the victim might have been, teeth can pinpoint race, age, lifestyle, diet, and sometimes occupation. The odontologist looks for spaces, chips, fractures, the angle of each tooth, caps, fillings, and missing or false teeth.

American Revolutionary hero Paul Revere is famous for his midnight ride. But he was also a dentist. In 1776, he identified the body of General Joseph Warren after Warren had been killed in the Battle of Bunker Hill. Paul Revere identified the body by the false teeth he had made for the general.

IMAGE OVERLAY OR SUPERIMPOSITION

Police have another way of making skeletons talk: *photographic superimposition*. The term sounds complicated, but it's actually quite simple.

Sometimes police believe they know who a skeleton once was. To confirm their suspicion, they can use a photo taken of the person while he was alive and project it onto a movie screen. Then pictures of the victim's skull are superimposed over the picture on the screen.

This process can also be done by projecting the images onto a television screen using two video cameras. One camera focuses on the skull. The other camera tapes a photo of the person the police think the skeleton used to be. If medical X rays are available, these can also be compared with the skull.

Using either method, the outline of the skull must fit into the outline of the face. The nasal bones, teeth, and eyes must fit perfectly. If it is the wrong person, something will not match. Perhaps the jaw lines will overlap. The forehead ridge might be too short, or the cheekbones might be too high. Only the image of the correct person will fit exactly over the image of the skull.

ARTISTS

We have all seen in the newspaper or on TV pictures of criminals the police are looking for. Or sometimes the pictures are of people who are missing. Who draws those pictures?

Sometimes the drawing is produced by a computer, but often a police artist does the work. There are approximately 250 forensic artists in the United States.

To create a picture of a perpetrator, an artist listens and draws while a witness or victim describes the person. Even if the observer's view lasted only a few seconds or was hindered by darkness, a helpful picture can be created. One study showed that a person only needs to see an attacker for one-fifth of a second to be able to recall his appearance.

While this may be true, stress affects people's minds. Some people can remember everything—even small details. Others

forget everything. Their minds go blank. Still others *think* they can remember—but their memory is wrong. When the perpetrator of a crime used a weapon, the victim (or even a witness) can often describe the weapon in detail, but can't remember anything about the perpetrator.

The perpetrator was probably the worst person in the frightened victim's life. To remember his face is like reliving the horrible event. The artist must ask good questions and listen carefully to get an image. The victim or witness may be in shock during the interview, so the artist must be sensitive and not add to the trauma. Many artists can reproduce the likeness of a suspect so accurately that the victim cries when he sees the drawing.

Although a few artists can complete a composite in fifteen to twenty minutes, the average drawing takes two to three hours. If the attack was violent or if the victim was terrorized, it might take six or more hours.

Some artists use a mug-shot book to help the victim or witness recall features of the attacker. Maybe the suspect had an unusually large nose or bushy eyebrows or thick lips. Some police departments use a kit designed for officers with no artistic ability. The kit provides plastic overlays of various facial features.

Probably the most famous sketches are those used in two recent cases. While the FBI was searching for the Unabomber between 1978 and 1996, an artist's sketch of the suspect was published in almost every newspaper in the nation. And after the bombing of the Federal Building in Oklahoma City in 1995, sketches of two suspects were circulated on TV and in newspapers. When one suspect was apprehended days after the bombing, he looked almost identical to the artist's sketch.

COMPUTER SOFTWARE

Special computer programs can produce a picture of a face by combining the various features selected by a witness. Skin tones, chins, noses, eyes, eyebrows, lips, and hairstyles and colors can all be changed on screen with the click of a button. Scars, warts, pimples, moles, and tattoos can be added.

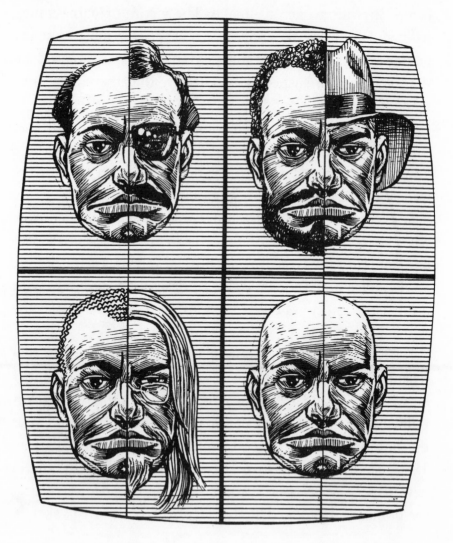

Some police departments have portable units that an officer can carry to a victim at the crime scene or in the hospital.

One advantage of computer-generated images is that appearances can easily be changed, allowing for multiple possibilities. Maybe the guy has grown a beard. Maybe he has shaved his beard off. Maybe he now wears glasses to disguise himself. Maybe he has changed his hairstyle or color. This is all quickly modified by the computer.

Another piece of computer software creates a face from a skull. When the measurements of the facial bones are entered, the computer fills in the tissue. A picture emerges on the screen of what the person might have looked like.

These computer programs are constantly being improved. Some are now available that look as realistic as photos.

Whether a sketch is done with clay or plastic overlays, by computer, or by an artist, its advantage is that it keeps the case in front of the public. Newspapers publish and TV programs broadcast the drawing in the hope that someone will recognize the suspect and come forward with helpful information.

AGE-ENHANCED PHOTOGRAPHS

Police try to solve old cases with *computer aging*. Using an old photo of a person, computer programs can "age" him. In cases of missing children, for instance, the computer can start with a child's preschool picture and suggest what he might look like ten or fifteen years later.

In 1971, a New Jersey man killed his mother, his wife, and his three children. Then he disappeared. For eighteen years the police could not find him.

Then the FBI created an age-enhanced photo of the wanted man, and it appeared in several publications. A woman recognized the photo as depicting her neighbor. She confronted the man's wife (his second wife), but she did not notify the authorities. Two years later, a television show profiled the case. This time a forensic artist had made a plaster model of the wanted man's head and shoulders. The model showed what the man probably looked like after eighteen years. It was presented along with the age-enhanced photo.

The same woman again recognized the suspect. He had moved from her neighborhood, but she knew his new address. This time she notified the FBI, and the man was apprehended. He is now in prison.

FASCINATING U.S. CRIME FACTS

About 60% of the murders in big cities are solved.

About 75% of the murders in small rural areas are solved.

About 87% of murder victims knew their killers.

According to one survey, 1 out of every 6 children ages 10 to 17 has seen or knows someone who has been shot.

U.S. CRIME CLOCK

A violent crime takes place every 17 seconds.

5

NOT-SO-DUMB ANIMALS

Anyone who owns a pet knows that animals communicate. Even a goldfish shows excitement when its owner approaches its bowl. So it's not surprising that animals, birds, and even insects can help solve crimes. But some animals are nothing short of amazing!

(While horses are not included in this chapter, many law-enforcement agencies have a mounted patrol. An officer on horseback is ten feet in the air and is intimidating, especially during a riot, a protest, or another crowd control situation. Horses are also used when officers need to get to remote, off-road locations, such as in mountainous terrain.)

DOGS

Ken-L Ration, a maker of dog food, gives an annual award for the most heroic dog in the United States. Many dogs have saved people from fires or from drowning. Along with these heroes, the company also makes awards to dogs that have protected their owners from criminals.

There was Meatball, a German shepherd from Alabama, who interrupted a burglary in progress at his family's greenhouse.

There was Chelsea, a golden retriever from Houston, Texas, who risked her life to save her master and a neighbor from two gunmen.

There was Sheena, a mixed-breed dog from St. Petersburg, Florida. Sheena rescued her disabled owner during an attempted robbery and assault in a supermarket parking lot.

There was 190-pound Lord Titan. He chased off a burglar and saved his mate, Miea, from a fire that the intruder had started. A few weeks later, Lord Titan and Miea became the proud parents of five puppies!

And there was King. The 100-pound German shepherd belonged to a seventy-seven-year-old man in Boston, Massachusetts. When a robber came to the apartment, King attacked. The intruder shot King in the neck, shoulder, thigh, and paw. But the dog did not give up his attack until the robber escaped out a window. King was awarded a gold medal for heroism.

K-9s

They're called K-9s. (It's a nickname for *canines*, which the dictionary defines as "animals of the dog family.") K-9s are highly trained dogs that work with law-enforcement officers. They are so intelligent that they seem smarter than many humans. Any dog lover understands how special a dog is. But police K-9s are extraordinary. They "come." They "stay." They "sit." They "heel." But even more, they find drugs, bombs, or a bad guy with a gun hiding in a building or in the woods.

Some dogs are trained for general police work. Others specialize: Some are drug sniffers; some sniff for firearms, others for explosives—especially at airports and on airplanes. Some seek out evidence of arson after a fire. Some locate fruits and meats brought into the United States

illegally. Dogs work at post offices, airports, military bases, and border crossings, as well as with police or sheriffs' officers. Drug-sniffing dogs are sometimes used in schools to reduce drug traffic.

Another type of specially trained dog is the search and rescue dog. When the Federal Building was bombed in Oklahoma City in 1995, search and rescue dogs with their handlers found many victims.

There are lots of advantages to having police dogs on the force:

- They work for food! They do not ask for pay raises, insurance, vacation, or retirement plans.

- Their size and agility allow them to go places where an adult person won't fit.

- Dogs run faster, go farther, and hear better than humans.

- A dog's sense of smell helps him search a building quickly and find things or people a human officer can't find. Narcotics detector dogs can check a car for drugs in two to five minutes. It would take a human twenty minutes. Explosives detector dogs find explosives in a fraction of the time a human would need, and the dogs have an accuracy rate of about 95 percent.

- Since a large, snarling dog is more frightening than a gun, dogs are often used for riot control.

- They save lives, assist in making arrests, and save millions of dollars of property.

A police dog will risk its life to attack anyone who is threatening its partner. The dog is the officer's pal . . . his partner on the job . . . his eyes in the dark . . . *and* a member of his family. The dog lives at home with his partner as part of the household.

K-9s and their handlers require about sixteen weeks of initial training. They learn voice commands and hand signals. While training a dog, an officer praises it when it does something right. When the dog makes a mistake, the punishment is usually a firm "No!" and sometimes a jerk on the leash. Handlers never physically punish their dogs.

On the job, the dog's reward is usually play and affection. He is rarely rewarded with food, since that could lead to an overweight dog!

Most K-9s are taught never to accept food from anyone except their handler or the family, as a criminal might try to poison the dog. One officer ran into a problem when he and his wife once went on vacation without the dog. (The dog usually went along.) For friends to be able to feed the dog, the officer had to touch (that is, leave his scent on) all the dog food before he left. Each day the friends would put the food in the garage without the dog's seeing them. The dog was then allowed into the garage to eat.

To be trained for police work, K-9s must be

intelligent, curious, healthy, and alert;

loyal to their handler-partner and willing to protect that partner without question;

large, powerful, agile, fast, and courageous;

gifted with a good sense of smell and a willingness to use it on command;

able to concentrate and not be distracted by noises, other animals, gunfire, or curious bystanders;

easily trained, responsive to commands, and under control at all times (K-9s must *stop* attacking on command); and

interested in fetching, if being trained as detector dogs.

Each training center has a different statistic, but one center reports that only one out of every 130 dogs is eligible to be a detector dog.

A law-enforcement dog will not attack without his partner's command *except* if the partner is attacked, if the dog himself is attacked, or if a suspect tries to escape. Still, if you ever encounter a police dog, do not approach the dog or try to pet it without asking the handler's permission.

Since male dogs are larger and stronger, they are used more often than female dogs. German shepherds are the most common breed, and the dogs are usually one to two years old when training begins.

Some police departments buy dogs that are already trained. The cost starts at about $6,500. Other departments accept donated dogs and have their own training programs.

Departments in large cities often prefer streetwise dogs from animal shelters. A homeless dog that has lived on city streets is not distracted by traffic, people, cats, noise, confusion, trash, and alleys crawling with rats. A dog that has been kept in a house or yard might be too curious to be properly trained.

The training never stops, and K-9s are tested once a year. There is even an annual event called the National Police Dog Trials to select the best K-9 dog in the United States.

BLOODHOUNDS

Some people think bloodhounds are vicious. Actually they are large but gentle dogs with great noses! One expert says that the average tracking dog has about 220 million scent receptors. Humans only have about 5 million.

A popular myth says that when a person walks through water, the water washes away his scent. That's not true. Dogs actually find bodies under water.

Bloodhounds can track fugitives as well as help find people who are lost. If a bloodhound finds a criminal, the testimony of the dog is admissible in court. The bloodhound is the only breed allowed that privilege.

Even if other officers find a fugitive before the dog can catch up, the dog needs to finish his trail and receive his reward. This will keep him excited about tracking.

In Colorado, a five-year-old girl was missing. After three days, Yogi, a bloodhound, joined the search. Yogi led his handler to an interstate highway and up a mountain canyon for fourteen miles, where searchers found the little girl's body.

PIGS

You might not find pigs working in your local police department, but it is possible to train pigs the same way dogs are trained.

A few law-enforcement agencies have experimented with Vietnamese potbellied pigs. As one pig owner said, "Pigs have been used to sniff for truffles in France for years. If they can find truffles, they can smell drugs."

There are advantages to working with pigs:

• They have an excellent sense of smell for sniffing out

illegal drugs. (A pig's sense of smell is second only to a bloodhound's.)

- The pig is the third-smartest land mammal. (Only humans and apes are smarter.)

- Pigs can be trained more quickly than dogs.

- They are friendly and loving.

- In small areas, their work is more accurate than a dog's.

- A pig's small body can squeeze into an area where a dog would not fit.

- Pigs are strong.

But there are also disadvantages:

- Pigs have one speed: very slow. If a large area (such as an entire building) is to be searched, it would take a pig forever to finish.

- Pigs make disgusting noises.

Pigs will never replace K-9 dogs. But some departments might find them useful and cost-effective as a weapon against drug trafficking.

BIRDS

Most birds just do bird things: fly, build nests, fly, hatch eggs, fly, and eat worms. But occasionally a bird becomes an important lead in a crime investigation—or even a star witness.

When a woman was killed in California, her business partner was charged with the murder. The woman's talking bird had witnessed the crime, and the suspect's lawyers believed the bird was trying to tell the authorities something. The bird kept saying, "Richard, no, no, no." The suspect was *not* named Richard. The court did not allow the bird's testimony in the trial, and the man was sentenced to life in prison. Was the bird just chattering? Or was it accusing another man of the murder? We may never know.

In a 1942 case, a man robbed and killed the owner of the Green Parrot Bar in New York City. Police questioned witnesses and looked for clues, but they couldn't solve the murder. The green parrot that lived at the bar kept saying, "Robber, robber, robber!" Everyone assumed the bird was repeating the owner's last words.

The parrot could say the names of the bar's regular customers, so one of the detectives decided to teach the parrot to say *his* name. He worked with the parrot for weeks before the bird could say his name. Suddenly the detective realized that the bird wouldn't be able to say "robber" after hearing the bar owner say it only once. Maybe the bird hadn't been saying, "Robber, robber, robber." What sounded similar? Perhaps "Robert"?

The detective discovered that one of the regular patrons had left town soon after the murder—and his name was Robert. The man was arrested in Baltimore, Maryland, and convicted of the murder. The story goes that when he was arrested, he said, "I never *did* like that bird."

In another case, when someone burglarized a house in Florida, a bird was stolen along with thousands of dollars' worth of possessions. After the burglary, the thief left the

bird at a tattoo parlor "for safekeeping." When a police officer stopped at the tattoo parlor, he heard a bird singing the theme song of *The Andy Griffith Show*. The officer remembered that the bird's owner had said his pet could sing that tune. Thanks to the bird's talent, the officer arrested a twenty-year-old man who confessed to the crime.

CATS

Cats sleep nineteen to twenty hours a day. They're not known for their guarding skills. How could they be any help in crime solving? They usually aren't, but there have been some amusing exceptions.

In Denver, Colorado, a two-year-old cat named Tiden-Taden lived at a grocery store. When a man tried to rob the store, the cat jumped on him and clawed him. Police broadcast a description of the suspect that included, "Probably has cat hairs on the coat and scratches on the face!"

A similar incident happened in Denver several years later. A cat named Melissa lived at a book and record store. When a man came into the store and attempted to rob the owner, Melissa attacked. By the time police arrived, Melissa had driven the attacker out.

In Wichita, Kansas, a woman came home from shopping to find her cat, Dumb-Dumb, restless. She let the cat out of the house and into the garage. Moments later she heard an "ungodly" noise and rushed to the door. Dumb-Dumb was biting and clawing the head of a man who had been trying to burglarize the family's house. The man screamed in pain and rushed from the garage. The cat didn't let loose until the man ran out of the yard.

BUGS

Bugs have roamed the earth for about 400 million years. But using bugs to help solve crimes has only recently become a common science.

The knowledge that flies are attracted to bodies is not new. In China in 1235, someone had murdered a victim using a sickle. The investigator knew that the killer could not have removed *all* traces of bodily evidence from his sickle. The investigator had all the local workers bring their sickles to him. After a few minutes, flies began to land on one of the blades. The flies proved that the owner of that sickle had committed the murder. The man confessed to the crime.

When a person or an animal dies, certain bugs are attracted to the body. Sound disgusting? It's the normal way of nature—part of the food chain. Within hours of a death, bugs come to feed on the flesh and to lay eggs—usually in the body's openings.

For years law-enforcement officers removed the bugs from bodies. They, too, found the bugs disgusting. The creepy crawly creatures seemed like destructive, grotesque, and repulsive nuisances. The field of forensic entomology has made police think again.

What can a bug contribute to a murder investigation? The answer is "Plenty!"

Picking bugs off dead bodies is not most people's idea of a good time, though, so there are

few forensic entomologists in the United States—probably fewer than two dozen. Entomologists study the insects on the body. They can often estimate the actual time of death within a few hours.

Common blowflies arrive at a murder scene first. They have a keen sense of smell and might come from a mile or more away. The flies lay thousands of eggs on the body. The eggs hatch into larvae in twelve hours to three days—depending on the species of the fly, the temperature, and the weather. The larvae are commonly known as maggots. Maggots can consume more than half of a victim's body.

Maggots go through three phases as they develop into adult flies. The entomologist tracks the development of the maggot and figures backward to determine the date and time the egg was probably deposited. This tells the time of the victim's death. Maggots are the best indicator an entomologist can use.

It can take from fourteen to twenty-five days for a blowfly to mature from egg to adult. The entomologist uses local temperature and humidity records, since maggots grow more slowly in cool temperatures, rain, or humidity.

Besides the blowfly, other flies are attracted to a body: houseflies, flesh flies, skipper flies, fruit flies, and coffin flies.

Then come the beetles: rove beetles, carrion beetles, clerid beetles, sap beetles, checkered beetles, scarab beetles, and dermestid beetles. And after the beetles come the wasps, spiders, mites, and moths.

Some of these insects come to feed on the body. Others come to feed on the insects that feed on the body.

The insects are attracted in a certain order, called *succession*. Knowing which insects are present when the body is discovered is another way an entomologist figures backward to know approximately how long the victim has been dead.

Some types of insects are city dwellers; others live in the country, and still others in the forest. If a body is found in the woods with city insects on it, the victim was probably killed in the city, then moved to the woods.

Certain bugs are attracted to bodies underwater. Finding the larvae of those insects on a body means that the body has been underwater.

Bugs can also give clues about drugs. If the body had cocaine in it, there will be cocaine in the bugs as well. In one Connecticut case, a woman's body was found inside a house a year after her death. An entomologist studied the dead bugs scattered near the remains. He determined that the woman had died from a drug overdose, since the chemicals had been passed on to the insects.

When a California woman's body was found in a field, the officers investigating the case developed red, scratchy welts on their legs. These welts were chigger bites. (Chiggers are a kind of mite larva.) Police questioned suspects and discovered that one man was covered with chigger bites. He said he was bitten in his backyard, but an entomologist determined that there were no chiggers in that neighborhood. Chiggers are rare in California. In fact, they were *only* found in the area where the body was discovered. The defendant had to have been at the scene where the body was found. The case was solved, and the man was found guilty of murder.

In another case, a man reported that his girlfriend had been murdered. It appeared that she had been killed by a burglar, as the windows were open in her apartment when the police arrived. At first the officers were puzzled, since there weren't any flies or maggots on the body. From this lack of flies, police soon concluded that the boyfriend had murdered the woman. After he had killed her, he left the windows closed with the air conditioner on. The next day he returned to the scene, opened the windows, and called the police.

There's a bright future in bugs. Crime investigators might soon do DNA tests on insects that take a blood meal. A mosquito at a murder scene might hold the blood of the person who committed the murder. Do a DNA test on the mosquito, match it to the DNA of the suspect, and you've already proved "whodunit"!

U.S. law-enforcement agencies make 14.6 million arrests each year (not including traffic violations).

Crime and violence in the United States cost $13.5 billion each year.

There are approximately 43,547,400 crime victims each year (*not* including murders).

There are 518,670 arrests each year for aggravated assault (an attack that intends bodily harm).

U.S. CRIME CLOCK

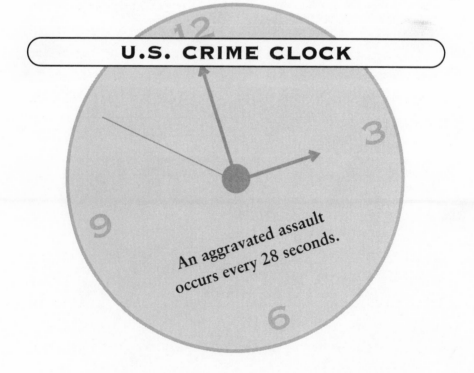

An aggravated assault occurs every 28 seconds.

6

DOWN TO EARTH

Dirt. Who would think it could help solve a crime? Or rocks? Or grass? Or snow?

More than a hundred years ago, the British writer Sir Arthur Conan Doyle made up a character for his books. The character was a detective named Sherlock Holmes. Sherlock Holmes solved crimes using methods that police were not yet using. In one story, the great detective could tell in which part of London someone had been walking by the mud on his trousers.

What a great idea! Soon the real police asked geologists to help solve cases. The geologists identified dirt and rocks and could tell where the minerals came from. With this information, crimes were solved.

Today, police often ask earth scientists for help in solving crimes.

DIRT

Call it *dirt*. Call it *soil*. Call it *earth*. Whatever you choose to name it, it can help the police.

Soil is distinctive. A sample from one piece of ground may be extremely different from one found just a short distance away. Geologists can identify the contents of the soil and tell where it came from. Detailed maps and charts help them. One expert estimates that there are fifty thousand varieties of soil in the United States. And that doesn't even include the variations of the identified varieties.

In a Wyoming case, a large amount of wool had been stolen after the sheep were sheared in the spring. A suspect was questioned, but he claimed that his wool was from sheep in another part of the state.

A geologist examined the soil from the scene of the theft and found that it was red shale and sandstone. Next he examined the soil from the area where the suspect claimed he had gotten his wool. The two soils were very different. Then the geologist examined the dust and soil on the wool. It was red shale and sandstone. The suspect was convicted of theft.

When a person kneels, sits, falls, or digs a hole (perhaps to bury a body), dirt gets embedded in his clothing and shoes and sometimes makes its way into pockets and pants cuffs. If a perpetrator has soil on his clothes, that soil might fall on the floor or furniture while he commits a crime. If a suspect is arrested with dirt on his clothes or in his vehicle, a geologist can determine whether the dirt came from the crime scene.

A few years ago, a woman's body was found in California. When a man was arrested for another murder, police found gravel in his car. A geologist identified the gravel as being unique and as matching the gravel used to bury the victim. The man, already convicted of another murder, is on death row.

Soil is transported by anything that moves, including animals or vehicles. Moisture causes soil to cling to the tires and to the metal, rubber, or plastic on the outside, inside, or bottom of a vehicle.

At the scene of a hit-and-run accident, dirt was jarred loose from the vehicle when it hit the victim. The dirt was on the highway when the state trooper arrived at the scene. A geologist said the dirt came from a lead-zinc mining district hundreds of miles to the south. When police arrested a suspect, his car had soil under the fenders that matched the dirt left at the crime scene. Police learned that the suspect had recently driven through the lead-zinc mining area.

In a recent case, Virginia authorities found an abandoned car belonging to a Pennsylvania police officer. But where was the officer?

Samples of soil taken from the car were sent to a geologist. The geologist and the police noted five important clues:

1. *A buildup of dirt in one wheel well and on the bumper.* This meant that the dirt was wet when it got on the car. Maybe someone got stuck in mud and spun the tire trying to get unstuck. Dirt in only one wheel well showed that the other wheel was still on the asphalt. The shoulder of the road must have been too narrow for the car to pull completely off the pavement.

2. *Yellow reflective paint in the dirt.* Yellow reflective paint on a road means a curve or a hill. It tells drivers not to pass. The car must have been stopped either near a curve or on a hill.

3. *Black slag.* In the winter, Pennsylvania highway crews use black slag from coal furnaces to prevent cars from skidding on curves or hills.

4. *Microfossils in limestone.* These particular fossils are found on a small strip of land that crosses a road south of Harrisburg, Pennsylvania.

5. *The missing man was heavyset.* Anyone trying to dispose of a large body would *not* drag it up a hill. He would look for a drop-off along the side of the road.

These clues led the authorities right to the road, the curve, the hill, and so to the police officer's body. The killer had dropped the body behind an embankment. It might never have been found without the help of the science of geology.

One of the most famous cases solved using geology was the Coors murder case in Colorado. Adolph Coors III disappeared one morning on his way to work. His automobile was found on the road leading out of his ranch. It was seven months before hunters found his body.

One month after Coors disappeared, a suspicious vehicle was found burning on a dump in New Jersey. Soil samples taken from under the car's fender showed four layers. The outer (last) layer was identified as soil from the dump. The second-youngest layer matched soil from the site where Coors's body was found. The third layer matched soil taken from the victim's ranch. The fourth and oldest layer was from the Denver area.

The owner of the burned vehicle was arrested. The soil evidence helped get a conviction for kidnapping and murder.

PLANTS

Like soil, plants vary from one location to another. A plant that grows in one type of soil might not survive in a different type a short distance away.

A 1942 murder case became famous as one of the first cases solved with plant evidence. On November 2, 1942, a

woman's body was found in Central Park in New York City. Her husband was questioned, and he claimed that he had been at a dance several blocks away at the time of her murder. Twenty-two women agreed that he had been there the entire time.

The police took the clothes that the man had been wearing the night of the murder. They discovered dirt in his trousers that matched the dirt where the body was found. And grass spikelets in his trouser cuffs matched grass spikelets at the murder scene.

The man insisted that he had not been in Central Park for two years. The grass must have been picked up somewhere else—perhaps in another park.

A professor of botany was consulted. He recognized the particular kind of grass as one that was rare in New York. The only place it grew in New York City was a small section of a hill in Central Park—the very hill where the murder had been committed.

Then the man suddenly remembered that he had gone through Central Park in September. But the professor said that the grass in question is a late bloomer. The spikelets found in the man's trouser cuffs could not have gotten there until *after* October 15. But they *could* have gotten there on November 1—the day the suspect's wife was murdered.

If the man had killed his wife anywhere else in the park, he might not have been caught. But the science of botany convicted him of murder.

Many parts of a plant can help the police—leaves, seeds, pollen, bark, or wood. They might be found in a vehicle, on clothing, in the hair, or on a weapon.

DNA testing can identify plants as positively as it identifies people. In a case in Arizona, a woman's body was found in the desert under a paloverde tree. Police arrested a man and found two paloverde seedpods in his pickup. DNA testing proved that the seedpods came from the specific tree under which the woman's body had been found. The evidence helped convict the man of murder.

A chair. A table. A ladder. They aren't plants, but if they are made of wood, they are considered plant material. Wood is excellent evidence if a piece (even a splinter) can be matched to a wooden object with that piece missing. Wood can also be analyzed for

the type of tree it is from (oak, walnut, pine, etc.);
the color and coarseness of the grain;
the existence of tool marks;
paints, stains, varnishes, or lacquers that may have been applied to the wood; and
any natural marks on the wood, such as the tree rings used to date the tree.

Probably the most famous case that used wood as evidence was the 1932 Lindbergh baby kidnapping. Charles Lindbergh became an American hero in 1927 when he flew solo in a single-engine plane from New York to Paris. Five years later, Charles and Anne Morrow Lindbergh's baby boy was kidnapped from his crib in the family's home.

One piece of evidence left at the scene was a wooden ladder. A wood expert proved by matching nail holes, growth rings, sawdust, and tool marks that the ladder rail had been made from a board taken from the suspect's attic. He also proved that the suspect's tools had been used to make the ladder. This and other evidence sealed the case. The suspect received the death sentence.

WEATHER

A store is robbed. The witness is knocked unconscious. When she regains consciousness, the police ask what time the robbery occurred. She can't remember, but there is one thing she does know: It had just started raining.

With this clue, the police can check with a local meteorologist and learn at exactly what time it started raining in that part of town.

Meteorologists record weather conditions, temperatures, wind speeds, wind direction, sun glare, movements of weather patterns, and even phases of the moon.

Weather information can be important. If police find a dead body, temperatures in the area will aid a medical examiner in knowing how quickly the body could be expected to decompose. Bug experts need weather and temperature information to know when insect eggs found on a body would hatch.

In cases such as automobile accidents, the angle of the sun at a certain time can determine who was at fault. Insurance claims often require a forensic meteorologist.

A popular story tells that while Abraham Lincoln was a country lawyer, the amount of light from the moon on a certain night helped him win a case. He proved that a witness could not have clearly seen the murder by the light of the moon.

Weather can provide important clues. In one case, police asked a man where he had been all evening. He said he had been home alone watching TV. But his coat was hanging over a chair dripping with water from the pouring rain outside.

In New York, police arrived immediately after a burglary had taken place. When they walked around the house, they found a single set of footprints in the snow. They followed the steps from the back door down the alley to a garage. Inside the garage, they found the perpetrator with the items he had stolen.

About 6% of all criminals commit 70% of all violent crimes.

Approximately 10% of all violent criminals each commit more than 600 crimes per year.

Those arrested for violent crimes average 9.4 arrests each.

There are 402,700 arrests made for burglary each year.

U.S. CRIME CLOCK

A burglary happens every 12 seconds.

7

FACT IS STRANGER THAN FICTION

Most criminals think they won't get caught. They think they're smarter than the police. If that were true, would our prisons be full? Would our court systems be overloaded? Studies have shown that the average IQ of a criminal is 90—about 10 points below that of an average member of the public.

STUPIDITY

A burglar in Wisconsin pulled off the perfect crime—almost. After robbing a woman's home, he called his mother long-distance on the woman's phone. Police didn't have a clue as to who had burglarized the house until the woman received her phone bill. The long-distance call was traced, and the man was arrested.

Police called a guy in Colorado the rocket scientist burglar because he would have had to be a rocket scientist to get out of this situation: The man removed his shoes, socks, and jacket and tried to slither down an air duct so he could rob a boutique. But he got stuck. The would-be burglar had to wait eleven hours, upside down, until the store employees arrived for work the next morning.

In California, a man burglarized a house, then returned to fix himself a snack and watch television. Had the man done a little reading, he would have realized that the house had been fumigated. Signs around the property warned of the poisonous fumes, and a tarpaulin covered the house to keep the vapors in. Police found the burglar on the lawn in front of the house, but he died from exposure to the poison soon after being taken to the hospital.

A hitchhiker in Connecticut robbed a motorist who had given him a ride. But when the hitchhiker got home, he discovered that the stolen wallet was empty. *Then* he realized he had left his own money pouch containing seventy dollars in the motorist's car.

So the hitchhiker called the guy who had given him a ride. They made arrangements to meet and exchange the stolen empty wallet for the forgotten money pouch. When the hitchhiker showed up, a detective was there to arrest him.

In Pennsylvania, a man burglarized a house, then called his dad to ask for a ride home. He didn't notice that he had tripped the answering machine and that it was recording his phone call. Police traced the call and arrested him.

And a bank robber in New York stuffed $2,100 into a brown paper bag and ran out of the bank. Surprise! Someone jumped out of a car, grabbed his bag of money, and drove off.

How did the bank robber respond? He did what any good citizen would do. He went to the nearest police station and reported that someone had stolen the money he had just robbed from a bank. He was promptly arrested!

GENEROSITY

When a man robbed a bank in California a week before Christmas, he dropped a dollar into a Salvation Army's donation kettle. Nice guy. The FBI confiscated the kettle to dust for fingerprints!

A fellow in New York City led police on a high-speed chase after he robbed a bank. The police couldn't believe their eyes as the guy started throwing the stolen money out his car window. About $6,300 of the cash was never recovered.

Similarly, a man in Chicago robbed a convenience store. Then, as police pursued him, he threw the money to people walking by.

When a guy in Las Vegas robbed a bank, he decided to share. He went outside and gave money to people eating lunch in the courtyard. To each person he encountered, he would say, "Have a nice day!" and hand out a hundred-dollar bill.

GHOSTS

In 1897 in a small West Virginia town, a young woman named Zona Heaster married a man known as Trout Shue. Three months later, Zona's body was found. The local doctor announced that Zona had died of an everlasting faint. The funeral was held, and Zona was buried.

Not long afterward, Zona's mother reported that on four nights, Zona's ghost had awakened her from sleep and accused Trout of killing Zona by breaking her neck.

Zona's body was brought up from her grave. An autopsy

confirmed that she had died from a broken neck and stran-
gulation. A trial was held, and Trout Shue was found guilty
of murdering his wife.

There have been many theories about the woman's death
in the years since the trial, and most authorities doubt the
ghost story.

More recently, another ghostly clue giver helped a Chicago
investigation. A woman had been murdered and a fire set in
her apartment. The police had no leads.

Months passed. Then a man called the police with an
odd story. The dead woman had spoken to him through
his wife. His wife had gone into a trance and, in a strange
voice, told the husband the dead woman's name and
details of the murder. She also told him the killer's name.
Some of the details the ghost had related were unknown to
the police. They checked the facts and found that they
were true.

Police found the killer, and he was convicted of murder.
The authorities are still puzzling over the source.

GOOD LUCK

Always wear your seat belts, folks!

Two men tried to rob a plumber in California by stopping
his van to ask for the time. When he looked down at his
watch, one of the men shot through the side window of the
van. The glass slowed the bullet, but the bullet was *stopped*
by the tightly woven nylon harness strap. If the plumber
hadn't been wearing his seat belt, the bullet would have
killed him.

In a somewhat similar incident, a man demanded money

from a retired New York City police officer. The officer gave the robber his money; then the robber shot the officer in the throat. *Luckily,* the bullet lodged in the officer's tie—saving his life!

BAD LUCK

From 1932 to 1948, an elderly man counterfeited money in the kitchen of his small New York City apartment. When he needed to buy food for himself or his dog, he made up a few one-dollar bills. The fake money was not very well done—he even misspelled Washington's name: Wahsington. He went to a different store each time and never passed more than one counterfeit bill at once.

One night there was a fire in his apartment. When firemen had extinguished the blaze, they piled his ruined belongings in the alley. Then it snowed and the snow covered everything.

The next day some boys were playing near the rubbish. They discovered bronze and copper plates and two counterfeit dollar bills. The authorities were notified, and the elderly man was arrested. It was later estimated that over the sixteen years, he had counterfeited five thousand dollars.

SLEEP

A California man broke into a woman's apartment and terrorized her. He found a bottle of pills and recklessly swallowed some. He should have read the label. They were sleeping pills. As soon as the man fell asleep, the woman called the police. Officers found their criminal sleeping soundly in the bathroom.

A New York man was convicted of burglary after police found him asleep in the victim's apartment with her jewelry in his pockets. The man had been arrested before when he fell asleep while burglarizing an office.

But a man in Ohio was *acquitted* of assault charges when he claimed he didn't know what he was doing: He had committed the crime while sleepwalking!

FASCINATING U.S. CRIME FACTS

There are 173,620 arrests made for robbery each year.

California has the most robberies, with more than 112,000 per year.

Poor households (families with yearly incomes less than $7,500) are victims of crime almost twice as often as upper-income households.

Vermont has the fewest robberies. One year the state had only 21.

U.S. CRIME CLOCK

A robbery is committed every 51 seconds.

8

HIGH TECH

Compu-cops. Robo-robbers. Cybercops. The far-out crime-solving fantasies of old science-fiction movies are now a reality on the streets of American cities.

COMPUTERS

Computers simplify police record-keeping systems. When there's a crime to solve, police can consider anyone who has ever been arrested in their jurisdiction by just pressing a few computer keys.

Laptop computers can go with an officer to roll call, to the patrol car, and to a crime scene. Forms and reports are simplified. An officer enters the arrest information and prints it in a fraction of the time the typewriter method required.

Questions about the law? Instead of carrying a complete law library, an officer can carry a software package that contains an entire state's law codes. The officer can retrieve legal information on any subject simply by striking a key.

The National Crime Information Center (NCIC) is an FBI computer system that allows law-enforcement agencies across the United States to share information. The system contains individuals' criminal histories, fingerprints, arrest warrants, and information on missing persons, firearms, and stolen property, and even data on people considered dangerous to the president of the United States.

PATROL CAR COMPUTERS

You don't really know the meaning of *static* until you've used a two-way radio. The sound quality is poor at best. And there isn't any privacy; anyone can use a police scanner to hear anything the officer and the dispatcher discuss. Besides, it often seems to take forever for a dispatcher to answer a call.

Instead, many police agencies have installed mobile data terminals. The officer gets information on a computer screen in the patrol car. There's no need to wait for a

dispatcher. No static. No more wondering who's listening to the conversation.

Now all the officer has to do is keep the patrol car on the road and read the computer screen at the same time!

A mobile data terminal increases police safety. The officer can check a license plate number to see if a vehicle is stolen. He'll know in about ten seconds and can request backup, since most people driving stolen cars are armed and dangerous.

Officers can also input the driver's license number and fingerprints of someone they have pulled over, to check the person's police record.

Maybe the best advantage: Most models have a red emergency button to push when there's trouble.

COMPUTER HEADS

No, that's not an insult. It's a new tiny computer that fits inside a police helmet. The chin strap contains the microphone. There's a video camera and a special screen that allows an officer to call up a criminal's record or the layout of a building he is approaching.

These five-ounce computers were designed for the military but are now available to law-enforcement agencies. They cost about nine thousand dollars each.

ON-LINE

With the click of a mouse, an officer is launched into cyberspace.

Virtual police stations on the Internet list missing children, show electronic mug shots, and provide neighborhood crime watch information.

Law-enforcement agencies know the value of help from the general public in solving crimes, so many agencies are using the Internet. The FBI has set up a site that contains its Ten Most Wanted Fugitives. For more information on the FBI, try its Internet address on the World Wide Web:

http://www.fbi.gov

Police departments with a page on the Web can share information about gang activities, firearm registrations, and stolen property. It's even possible to attend conferences on-line.

DNA FINGERPRINTING

One little drop of blood or saliva is all it takes to tell you from 23 million other people. Even dried blood or dried saliva on a telephone receiver can be used to do a DNA profile.

DNA stands for deoxyribonucleic acid. Identifying DNA is as complicated as spelling its name! Here's how it's done:

1. A blood sample is taken from a suspect.

2. White blood cells are removed from the blood sample.

3. One white blood cell is burst open to release the DNA strands.

4. The strands are snipped into pieces using enzymes called *restriction enzymes*.

5. The fragments are placed on a sheet that has been coated with a special gel.

6. An electric current is used in a process called *electrophoresis* to separate the DNA fragments into a pattern of bands.

7. The bands are transferred to a nylon sheet.

8. The nylon sheet is exposed to mildly radioactive probes. Each probe binds to a specific DNA sequence in the bands. (This step allows scientists to focus on the areas they want to use to identify someone.)

9. The nylon sheet is placed against a piece of X-ray film.

10. The X-ray film is developed, and out comes a DNA reading. (The reading looks sort of like the bar code used for electric scanning of prices at the grocery store.)

11. The DNA of a suspect is then compared with the DNA of evidence found at a crime scene.

Dr. Alec Jeffreys, a scientist in England, discovered the DNA testing method in 1984. He found that every cell in a person's body contains DNA. And the DNA in a person's blood makes the same DNA print as a cell from his skin, hair root, tooth pulp, bone marrow, urine, saliva, sweat, or any other body fluid.

The cells form a pattern called a *DNA fingerprint*. No two people have the same DNA—except identical twins.

In 1983, a man in Virginia was attacking women. Suddenly

the attacks stopped. Four years went by. In 1987, the attacks began again and four women were killed.

One detective figured that maybe the killer had been in jail during the four years when there were no attacks. He went through the list of men recently released. When one suspect was arrested, his DNA matched the DNA on body fluids found at one of the crime scenes.

The man was tried and convicted and became the first person in the United States to be executed as a result of DNA evidence.

A *locus* is a place or a location. Everyone's DNA has about 3 billion loci (the plural of *locus*). Those loci tell us that a certain person has one heart, two ears, ten toes, and so on. The traits everyone shares have identical DNA codes.

DNA differs when one person has black hair while another is a redhead. One person is tall; another, short. One has brown eyes; another, blue. Each person has a difference at 10 million spots along the DNA strand. That means that about one in every three hundred loci will be unique. These points of individuality are called *DNA markers*.

In 1993, the World Trade Center in New York City was bombed and six people were killed. A terrorist sent a letter to *The New York Times* claiming responsibility. After a suspect was arrested, the FBI compared his DNA with the DNA from the saliva used to seal the envelope. They matched!

In the Unabomber case, the FBI developed a DNA profile of the saliva from a postage stamp on a letter the perpetrator mailed in 1995. When a suspect was arrested a year later, the lab profiled DNA from saliva on a letter the suspect had sent to his brother. The two profiles matched.

There are disadvantages to DNA testing. Traditional blood tests are done quickly in small labs. DNA tests must be sent to labs with special equipment. Those labs often take a long time to process the evidence. (Meanwhile, the wrong person might sit in jail while the bad guy gets away with murder.)

DNA testing (one hundred dollars per sample) costs fifty to a hundred times more than traditional blood testing. Often police take as many as 150 blood samples from a crime scene. It would cost fifteen thousand dollars to do DNA testing on all those samples.

The greatest *advantage* is the accuracy of DNA fingerprinting. The chance of two people's having identical DNA is between one chance in 5 million and one chance in 47 million.

DNA tests can prove innocence as well as guilt. A man in Virginia was in prison for murdering a lawyer. When DNA testing became available, the man was found to be innocent. He was released after serving five years for a crime he did not commit.

In 1996, a California man was released from prison after serving *sixteen* years for beating his wife and killing their unborn baby. After a DNA test showed that the man was innocent, the judge told him, "You're about to wake up after a sixteen-year nightmare. You may exit the building through any door you like."

SMART GUNS

Researchers have tried to make *smart guns* for years. The idea is that an officer's gun would not work for anyone except the officer. If a criminal grabbed the gun during a struggle, it wouldn't shoot. Experts estimate that 15 percent of officers killed in the line of duty are shot with their own weapons. Smart guns would prevent such a situation.

The added advantage would be home safety. If the officer's child got hold of and played with his gun at home, the child would not be able to accidentally fire it.

Goop Gun

Some call it sticky foam . . . or goo . . . or goop . . . or slime. It's a nonhardening plastic foam shot from a shoulder-slung

exterminator's gun. The extra-sticky substance wraps a suspect in long strings that prevent movement. Goop guns would be effective for riot control.

The weapon's advantages? It doesn't kill anyone! It disables a suspect so that he can't fight or resist. Its disadvantage? It is extremely difficult to clean up. The gooey stuff gets all over everything, including the officer.

It might be a while before your local police department uses sticky foam. The cost is high, and the product is still being refined for law-enforcement use.

NETS

Imagine a police officer reeling in a criminal the same way a fisherman catches a tuna. The device is called the net.

After being shot from a handheld baton or from an attachment on a shotgun, a canister explodes and releases a net. The net wraps around a suspect in less than a second. That suspect isn't going anywhere until the officer decides he is!

LASERS

The word *laser* is an acronym (a word formed by the first letters of a series of words) for "light amplification by stimulated emission of radiation." A laser produces a narrow, intense beam of light. The light is concentrated—it does not spread.

Some traffic cops use lasers to determine how fast vehicles are going. The result: more speeding tickets!

For police investigating a crime scene, a laser can pick up fingerprints that can't be found by powder or chemical techniques. These prints might be on glass, paper, cloth, cardboard, rubber, wood, plastic, leather, or even human skin.

A laser can also illuminate hair, fiber, and body fluids that are invisible to the naked eye.

The argon laser was developed for use by the military. When a body was found in Georgia in 1983, police couldn't gather fingerprint evidence until they used an argon laser. Under the pencil-thin, bluish beam of light, prints showed up immediately on a plastic garbage bag at the scene. The police made an arrest.

LIE DETECTORS

Centuries ago in East Asia, if a person was suspected of lying, he was given some rice to chew. If he could spit it out, he was innocent. If it remained dry and he could not spit, he was guilty. It was believed that fear caused by a person's guilt would dry up his saliva.

Today's law-enforcement agencies don't use rice! They use a machine called the polygraph. To operate the polygraph, tubes are placed around the waist of the subject to measure his rate of breathing. A metal plate placed on his hand measures perspiration. And a cuff fastened around his arm monitors his heartbeat and blood pressure.

While the person giving the test asks yes-or-no questions, a paper rolls through the machine. Ink lines on the paper record the body's reactions.

To begin, the subject is asked simple questions, such as, "Is your name Herman Smith? Are you thirty-five years old?" The machine is thus able to record the person's normal body reactions. When questions about the crime are

asked, the lie detector measures differences in the body's reactions. Does the subject's hand suddenly start to sweat when he's asked if he robbed the First National Bank?

It is estimated that 9 to 12 million people take polygraph tests each year.

Critics of the machines call them "stress tests" or "fear detectors." They say the tests measure anxiety, not truthfulness. An honest person who is under a lot of stress could fail the test. What if the police were then to stop looking for the real criminal?

Examiners who have used lie detectors for many years defend the machines. They say the polygraph is 85 to 90 percent accurate *if* the test is conducted by a skilled tester.

One advantage of the polygraph is a psychological one. A suspect who is asked to take a lie detector test often confesses just before taking the test, during the test, or afterward when he is told that he failed.

The results of a polygraph test are not allowed as evidence in most courts in the United States.

NIGHT VISION

Night vision goggles were originally designed for military helicopter pilots.

Some models use infrared, which works by detecting heat. A tracking device searches out the heat of a person hidden in darkness. It can even show the heat from tires that have just left the scene of a crime—allowing officers to trail the perpetrator.

Another type of night vision takes any light available—streetlights, moonlight, even starlight—and amplifies it thirty thousand to fifty thousand times. Suddenly night becomes as bright as day.

Various models of night vision products are available: goggles, binoculars, monoculars, pocket scopes, weapon sights, and video cameras, as well as other highly specialized equipment.

Photo Enhancement or Image Enhancement

When the space shuttle *Challenger* exploded in 1986, the National Aeronautics and Space Administration (NASA) used image enhancement to study the pictures of the explosion. That same technology helps police solve crimes.

When a champion figure skater was attacked in Detroit, three different people caught the incident on videotape. The tapes were enlarged and digitally enhanced, meaning that a computer assigned a number code to each shade of gray in a black-and-white version of the tape. The computer could then eliminate certain shades to remove the blur from the picture and make the image sharp.

A similar incident occurred in New Mexico after a bank robbery. The pictures from the bank's surveillance camera were hazy. A lab used computer enhancement to bring the photos into focus. One officer said that he could then even read the printing on one perpetrator's T-shirt. With the enhanced photos, an arrest was soon made.

Robots

He's the newest cop on the force.

His first year he costs a hundred and fifty thousand

dollars, but he never asks for a pay increase, health insurance, or a pension plan. He's three feet tall and weighs 275 pounds, but without an ounce of fat! He can only go one or two miles an hour, but his grip can crush a man's hand. His arm can rotate 360 degrees, and his eyes, like an expensive camera, can zoom in on a scene.

His name is Robot, and he saves his fellow officers' lives.

Robots are often part of a Special Weapons and Tactics (SWAT) team. They are used in various ways:

- to approach barricaded suspects

- on bomb squads to retrieve, dismantle, or remove bombs

- to enter and videotape areas occupied by armed people

- to deliver food or telephones (allowing for negotiation) in hostage situations

- to fling tear gas grenades through windows

- to enter areas where hazardous materials have been spilled

A robot is usually transported in a police van. Its handler is trained to operate the robot by remote control. Batteries or an electrical cable provide its power.

A robot is capable of numerous maneuvers, including going up or down stairs, peering through windows with a video camera, and shooting a shotgun, stun gun, or water cannon. Robots can move an object or person weighing up to 350 pounds. They can also open doors with a key or turn doorknobs, though if the door swings toward the robot, it might take him as long as thirty minutes to get inside! Some robots carry X-ray devices, microphones, high-intensity lights, gas analyzers, infrared cameras, or cameras with zoom lenses.

The biggest problem with robots is their price. A robot costs between forty thousand and one hundred and seventy thousand dollars, depending on its accessories.

In Texas, a young man was barricaded in an apartment. The police sent in a robot with a camera to scan the interior. When

the suspect saw the robot, he gave up and came out, yelling, "What in the !@*!#*@ kind of machine is that?"

In Elmira, New York, two robbery suspects had killed one officer and wounded two others. The police didn't want to risk having more officers shot. So a 230-pound robot named RMI-3 went into the house and scanned the room with its video camera eyes. It pushed debris aside and found that the two gunmen were dead.

For its bravery, RMI-3 was awarded the honor of Cop of the Month. At the ceremony, the robot went forward and extended its arm to receive its plaque from the police commissioner. It then turned around and showed its award to the audience. When asked later what he thought the robot was thinking, the commissioner said, "I hope he's *not!*"

ANNE DROID

If the name sounds like that of one of your long-lost cousins, think again! Anne Droid is a new security device.

She's a department store mannequin that looks like any other mannequin, modeling the latest clothing styles. But her eye is actually a video camera, and there's a microphone up her nose. Thieves beware!

Shoplifters pocket $35 million worth of merchandise per day in the United States. Anne Droid plans to cut those figures.

STOP STICK

It might sound like a game for kids, but Stop Stick is actually a crime-fighting device. It's a piece of plastic that stretches out to nine feet. Its thirty-six sharp spikes can be raised or lowered instantly. When the Stop Stick is dropped in front of a vehicle during a high-speed chase, the spokes go into the tires, letting the air out—slowly, so that the driver does not lose control of his vehicle.

VIDEO CAMERAS

Video cameras—they're not just for home movies anymore!

Video cameras are used in surveillance at banks, convenience stores, and other businesses. If the business is robbed, the camera has a picture of the perpetrator.

Video cameras are also used to tape a crime scene before any evidence has been moved. If another detective joins the case at a later date, the video is available to him.

Videos are also used in police training, on robots, on K-9s, and in patrol cars.

In 1991, a constable in a small Texas town stopped a car for a traffic violation. With his own money, the officer had recently purchased a video camera for his patrol car. The camera was running when the constable approached the vehicle. In the minutes that followed, the three men killed the officer, then fled.

The video camera had recorded the entire murder, giving authorities pictures of the men responsible. Within days the men were captured. They were tried and convicted of murder.

AND MORE

Technology gets better every day. It seems amazing that police could catch even one criminal a hundred years ago.

Here are more innovative ideas that some police departments are trying:

- **Global positioning satellite (GPS) network.** Satellites orbiting the earth provide police dispatchers with the exact location of each police car.

- **Video imaging technology.** Instead of posing for a "still" picture, the suspect stands in front of a video camera that's connected to a computer. His image is projected on the computer monitor and can be saved.

- **Voice stress analyzer.** Similar to the polygraph, this machine measures stress in the voice.

- **Radar detector detector.** Traffic officers use radar guns to clock a vehicle's speed. To avoid speeding tickets, some drivers install illegal radar detectors. Now officers have machines that can detect radar detectors!

- **Strobe.** A strobe is an extremely bright light that pulses. The pulsing light disorients a suspect. Officers must wear special goggles when they use the strobe to take a suspect into custody. One person who tested the strobe felt as if he were a second behind the rest of the world. "I couldn't even catch a ball," he said.

- **Sound stunner.** This tool works on the same principle as the strobe, except that it uses pulsating *sounds* instead of lights.

- **Radio engine disabler.** This device sends a signal that disables a car so that high-speed chases can be avoided.

- **Tracing pellets.** Small radio transmitters placed in tiny pellets are shot into a getaway car. Police can discontinue a high-speed chase, then later follow the radio transmissions to track the car.

- **LifeGuard.** This is not pool police or beach patrol. It's a computer linked to a TV camera. It locates a bullet after it has been fired but before it hits its target. Snapping two hundred pictures per second, the computer traces the bullet's path back to where it was fired from. It can trace up to ten bullets at once. There are also other brand names.

A computer won't stop a drug addict from robbing a bank. A satellite system won't prevent a mass murderer from shooting people. All the modern gadgets won't cut the crime rate.

Or will they?

With the latest technology in place, the police can solve old cases. And each arrest can be said to "solve" the cases that the criminal is no longer able to commit.

Computer fingerprint systems can often identify a suspect so quickly that an arrest is made even before a detective is assigned. Thousands of unnecessary case-solving hours are saved—and the criminal is off the streets thousands of hours earlier.

About 80% of people arrested are male.

Approximately 70% of all arrests are men ages 15 to 34.

About 40% of all arrests are men ages 15 to 24.

There are 19,400 arrests made for arson each year.

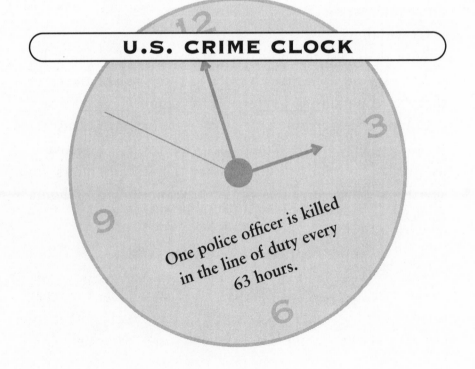

U.S. CRIME CLOCK

One police officer is killed in the line of duty every 63 hours.

9

EASIER SAID THAN DONE

Computers, smart guns, talking bones. It seems as if police should be able to solve crimes with little time and effort.

While detectives on television solve crimes in one hour, we all know that real life doesn't work that way. As one officer said, "I wish it were as easy as TV makes it look."

IF COPS ARE SO SMART, WHY ARE THERE UNSOLVED CRIMES?

Solving a crime is a difficult job. Some of the stories in this book might make it sound easy, but it rarely is. Despite all the advances in forensic science and technology, problems remain.

There are approximately seventeen thousand law-enforcement agencies in the United States. About 90 percent of those agencies have twenty-four or fewer officers. About 80 percent of the agencies have fewer than twenty officers. Almost half have fewer than ten.

Small departments do not have enough staff to use high-tech devices. The officers must spend their time on rounds rather than in the office. What's more, small-town officers usually don't receive the training in detective work that city officers get. Some small communities have only one

murder in a ten-year span. It makes sense to put the limited budget money into the problems the officers address daily.

COST

Technology is e-x-p-e-n-s-i-v-e! Much of the crime-solving equipment described in this book costs more than small law-enforcement agencies can afford. And even in large departments, budgets are cut and tax dollars are not available for new equipment. A sudden crime increase can drain a police department's resources.

Further, buying the original equipment is not the only cost. Some devices need a special setup or work space—laboratory sinks, exhausts for fumes, high-voltage electricity, running water to cool units, liquid nitrogen, or a darkened area for photography. And some equipment requires the purchase of component parts, as well as constant testing to guarantee accuracy.

No Evidence or Suspect

Lack of evidence is another reason crimes sometimes go unsolved. The crime might not have been discovered until the evidence had been destroyed. Evidence might have been improperly handled. Or witnesses and medical personnel might have contaminated the evidence in the process of assisting a victim or viewing a crime scene.

Still, police can have the best evidence in the world, but until they have a suspect, it doesn't do them any good. They can have a perfect fingerprint to run through AFIS, but if the perpetrator's prints are not on file, AFIS can't make a match. They can have a bullet or a bite mark, but without a suspect, there is nothing to prove.

The most important part of crime solving is good police work. Cleverness and common sense are the links that make the evidence speak.

There are 195,900 arrests made for motor vehicle theft each year.

The first police department to use an automobile was in Akron, Ohio, in 1899.

About 90.5% of law-enforcement officers are male.

The first murder in the colonies that later became the United States occurred at Fort Amsterdam in New York in 1638.

U.S. CRIME CLOCK

One larceny (theft) is committed every 4 seconds.

GLOSSARY

AFIS: Automated Fingerprint Identification System.

AUTOPSY: The examination of a body to determine the cause and time of death.

BOTANIST: A scientist who studies plant life.

ENTOMOLOGIST: A scientist who studies insects.

FORENSIC: Applying a scientific knowledge to questions of law.

FORENSIC ANTHROPOLOGIST: A scientist who studies the physical characteristics of humans and the remains of the dead for details of their past life, as well as the cause of their death.

FORENSIC ARTIST: An artist who specializes in facial reconstruction.

FORENSIC MEDICINE: A science that applies medical knowledge to legal and criminal issues.

GEOLOGIST: A scientist who studies the earth's crust and its interior, rocks, and fossils.

LAB TECHNICIAN: A person who works in a scientific laboratory using technical equipment and procedures.

LATENT: Refers to something invisible to the naked eye, such as a fingerprint or shoe print.

METEOROLOGIST: A scientist who studies the atmosphere and weather.

ODONTOLOGIST: A scientist who studies teeth, bite marks, and dentures. A forensic odontologist applies knowledge of teeth to obtain criminal evidence, identify physical remains, or identify the source of bite wounds.

PATHOLOGIST: A medical doctor who studies diseases and injuries and their causes and consequences. Also, a doctor who examines the soft tissue of bodies after a crime.

PERPETRATOR: A person who commits a crime.

POLYGRAPH: A lie detector machine.

STRIATIONS: A series of parallel lines of varying width, depth, and separation; scratch marks on the surface of a bullet.

SURVEILLANCE: The observation of a person, place, or thing by a person or a camera.

PLACES TO VISIT

AMERICAN POLICE CENTER & MUSEUM
1717 SOUTH STATE STREET
CHICAGO, ILLINOIS 60616-1215
ADMISSION CHARGE

AMERICAN POLICE HALL OF FAME AND MUSEUM
3801 BISCAYNE BOULEVARD
MIAMI, FLORIDA 33137
ADMISSION CHARGE

CLEVELAND POLICE HISTORICAL SOCIETY, INC., AND MUSEUM
JUSTICE CENTER
1300 ONTARIO STREET
CLEVELAND, OHIO 44113
FREE ADMISSION

CRIMINAL JUSTICE HALL OF FAME
5400 BROAD RIVER ROAD
COLUMBIA, SOUTH CAROLINA 29210
FREE ADMISSION

J. EDGAR HOOVER FBI BUILDING—PUBLIC TOUR
10TH STREET AND PENNSYLVANIA AVENUE, NORTHWEST
WASHINGTON, D.C. 20535
FREE ADMISSION

PHOENIX POLICE MUSEUM
BARRISTER PLACE BUILDING
101 SOUTH CENTRAL AVENUE, SUITE 100
PHOENIX, ARIZONA 85004
FREE ADMISSION

PORTLAND POLICE MUSEUM
JUSTICE CENTER
1111 S.W. SECOND AVENUE
PORTLAND, OREGON 97204
FREE ADMISSION

TEXAS RANGER MUSEUM & HALL OF FAME
EXIT 335 B, I-35 AND UNIVERSITY PARKS
P.O. BOX 2570
WACO, TEXAS 76702-2570
ADMISSION CHARGE

"WHODUNIT? THE SCIENCE OF SOLVING CRIME"
A TRAVELING EXHIBIT THAT WILL BE APPEARING IN SCIENCE
    MUSEUMS IN MAJOR CITIES ACROSS AMERICA, SPONSORED BY:
FORT WORTH MUSEUM OF SCIENCE AND HISTORY
1501 MONTGOMERY STREET
FORT WORTH, TEXAS 76107
ADMISSION CHARGE

ODDS 'N' ENDS

National Police Week is celebrated in mid-May every year. Send a self-addressed stamped envelope for free information:

Police Week Information
American Police Hall of Fame
3801 Biscayne Boulevard
Miami, Florida 33137

Are you interested in a career in forensic science? The Forensic Sciences Foundation, Inc., has a Career Brochure it will send *while supplies last*. Or if you have a specific question, the foundation will try to answer it:

Forensic Sciences Foundation, Inc.
P.O. Box 669
Colorado Springs, Colorado 80901-0669

Thinking about a law-enforcement career? Young adults (ages fourteen to twenty) are eligible to join an Explorer Post, a division of the Boy Scouts of America. There are approximately 2,200 law-enforcement Explorer Posts across the country open to both males and females. Contact your local Boy Scout Council for information. If you can't find your local office, write to the following address and the Scouts will tell you whom to contact:

Boy Scouts of America
1325 West Walnut Hill Lane
P.O. Box 152079
Irving, Texas 75015-2079

OTHER BOOKS YOU'LL ENJOY

Bone Detectives, by Donna Jackson (Boston: Little, Brown, 1996).

Crime Lab 101, by Robert Gardner (New York: Walker & Co., 1992).

Law Enforcement Dogs, by Phyllis Raybin Emert (New York: Crestwood House, 1985).

SELECTED BIBLIOGRAPHY

Bodziak, William J. *Footwear Impression Evidence.* New York: Elsevier, 1990.

Catts, E. Paul, and Neal H. Haskell, editors. *Entomology and Death: A Procedural Guide.* Clemson, South Carolina: Joyce's Print Shop, 1990.

Crime in the United States, 1994. Washington, D.C.: U.S. Department of Justice, 1995.

Donigan, Robert L., Edward C. Fisher, Robert H. Reeder, and Richard N. Williams. *The Evidence Handbook.* Evanston, Illinois: The Traffic Institute, Northwestern University, 1975.

F.B.I. Law Enforcement Bulletin. Numerous articles.

Fisher, Barry A. J., Arno Svensson, and Otto Wendel. *Techniques of Crime Scene Investigation*, 4th edition. New York: Elsevier, 1987.

Fisher, David. *Hard Evidence.* New York: Simon & Schuster, 1995.

Handbook of Forensic Science. Washington, D.C.: Federal Bureau of Investigation, 1995.

Journal of Forensic Sciences. Numerous articles.

Macdonald, John, and Tom Haney. *Criminal Investigation*. Denver, Colorado: Apache Press, 1990.

Maples, William R., and Michael Browning. *Dead Men Do Tell Tales*. New York: Doubleday, 1994.

McDonald, Peter. *Tire Imprint Evidence*. New York: Elsevier, 1989.

McPhee, John. "Annals of Crime," *The New Yorker*. January 29, 1996, p. 44.

Moenssens, Andre A., Ray Edward Moses, and Fred E. Inbau. *Scientific Evidence in Criminal Cases*. Mineola, New York: The Foundation Press, 1973.

Murray, Raymond C., and John C. F. Tedrow. *Forensic Geology*. New Brunswick, New Jersey: Rutgers University Press, 1975.

The New York Times. Numerous references.

NewsBank. New Canaan, Connecticut: CD News from NewsBank: 1985–1996. Numerous articles.

O'Hara, Charles E., and Gregory L. O'Hara. *Fundamentals of Criminal Investigation*. Springfield, Illinois: Charles C. Thomas, 1994.

Osterburg, James W. *Criminal Investigation*. Cincinnati, Ohio: Anderson Publishing, 1992.

Shook, Michael D., and Jeffrey D. Meyer. *Legal Briefs*. New York: Macmillan, 1995.

Sifakis, Carl. *Encyclopedia of American Crime*. New York: Facts on File, 1982.

The Science of Fingerprints. Washington, D.C.: United
States Department of Justice, 1984.

Wrobleski, Henry M., and Karen M. Hess. *Introduction to
Law Enforcement and Criminal Justice*, 4th edition. St.
Paul, Minnesota: West Publishing, 1993.

INDEX